CALLED AND ACCOUNTABLE

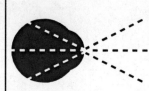

This Large Print Book carries the
Seal of Approval of N.A.V.H.

CALLED AND ACCOUNTABLE

DISCOVERING YOUR PLACE IN GOD'S ETERNAL PURPOSE

TENTH ANNIVERSARY EDITION

HENRY T. BLACKABY
NORMAN C. BLACKABY

THORNDIKE PRESS
A part of Gale, Cengage Learning

GALE
CENGAGE Learning·

Detroit • New York • San Francisco • New Haven, Conn • Waterville, Maine • London

GALE
CENGAGE Learning®

LIBRARY OF CONGRESS CATALOGING-IN-PUBLICATION DATA

Blackaby, Henry T., 1935–
    Called and accountable : discovering your place in God's eternal purpose / by Henry T. Blackaby and Norman C. Blackaby. — 10th anniversary ed., Large print ed.
        p. cm. — (Christian Large Print originals)
        Originally published: Birmingham, AL : New Hope Publishers, c2012.
        ISBN 978-1-59415-443-0 (softcover) — ISBN 1-59415-443-0 (softcover) 1. Christian life — Textbooks. 2. Christian life — Baptist authors. 3. Large type books. I. Blackaby, Norman C. II. Title.
    BV4740.B57 2012b
    248.4—dc23
                                                                    2012021054

Published in 2012 by arrangement with New Hope Publishers.

Printed in the United States of America
    1 2 3 4 5   16 15 14 13 12

FD212

Dedication

To my uncle and his wife, *Lorimer* and *Olive Baker,* who faithfully served as missionaries in Manchuria, China, working with Jonathon Goforth during the great Shantung Revival, and who baptized me as a nine-year-old boy and later became my pastor when God called me into the ministry.
HENRY BLACKABY

To my wife, Dana, with gratitude to our Lord, for your love and support.

and

To our three children — *Emily, Douglas,* and *Anne* — our fellow partners in living out God's call on our family.
NORMAN BLACKABY

TABLE OF CONTENTS

BEFORE YOU BEGIN

Your study of this book can be a wonderful time of deepening your relationship with God. We pray that as you begin this encounter with God you will consider several things:

1. *Consider* enlisting a prayer partner who will pray for you during the six-week study.
2. *Notice* there are testimonies provided along with each unit. These testimonies will help you see how other Christians, historical and modern-day, have understood and lived their place in God's eternal purpose.
3. *Notice* that the study is designed to guide you through five days of study each week. Please use the other two days to reflect on what God has spoken to you through the five days of guided study.

4. *Remember,* this is a time to encounter God, not simply to complete a study.

SMALL-GROUP OR INDIVIDUAL STUDY?

The study can be done in a small group or as an individual study. However, if a group decides to go through the study together, there are a few guidelines provided for the leader in the Leader's Guide, found in the back of this book. Encourage individuals to complete each unit before you meet, then at your weekly group meeting, give the group time to share what God is teaching them. Make sure you save time to pray together as God guides the group to know and experience that all are *Called and Accountable!*

CALLED AND ACCOUNTABLE:

Discovering Your Place in God's Eternal Purpose Tenth Anniversary Edition DVD

- The DVD segments complement the content contained within your six-week study.
- Six 15- to 30-minute teaching segments with content presented by Norman Blackaby can be viewed before or after studying each respective unit in this study.
- The DVD also provides retrospective vignettes with Henry and Norman sharing how this classic study has had an impact on individual believers, helping each person find his or her place in God's eternal purpose.
- Whether you use this study with or without the DVD, you will gain a pointed study that enables believers to focus on the search for answers to key

questions about God's calling on a believer's life. If you are a participant in a study with the DVD, you will find the Participant/Viewer Notes pages in the back a helpful tool to jot notes while viewing the DVD.

INTRODUCTION

It is overwhelming to realize that the God of the universe, the only God and Creator of all that is, has chosen to call every believer into a very special relationship with Himself. This call and the relationship that follows are very personal! The truth of this is found on almost every page of the Bible, in life after life, and verse after verse. It is central to the entire message of the Bible. It is, in fact, an expression of the very heart of God. Even more amazing is the knowledge that it was God's choice to call people into such a personal relationship with Himself: "He chose us in Him [Christ], before the foundation of the world, to be holy and blameless in His sight" (Ephesians 1:4 NIV). Jesus expressed this plan of the Father to His disciples this way: "You did not choose Me, but I chose you. I appointed you that you should go out and produce fruit, and that your fruit should remain, so that whatever you ask the Father in My name, He will give you" (John 15:16 HCSB).

This truth remains to this day, and includes each of us. When this truth grips a person's heart, he or she is never the same again. Immediately there comes into that life a deep sense of meaning and purpose, and a sense of stewardship, or accountability, to God. So personal and real was this truth to David that he said to God,

My frame was not hidden from You,
When I was made in secret,
And skillfully wrought in the lowest parts of the earth.
Your eyes saw my substance, being yet unformed.
And in Your book they all were written,
The days fashioned for me,
When as yet there were none of them.
How precious also are Your thoughts to me,
O God!
How great is the sum of them!
If I should count them, they would be more in number than the sand;
When I awake, I am still with You.
— PSALM 139:15–18

Jeremiah also was made aware of this when God informed him that:

Before I formed you in the womb I knew you;
Before you were born I sanctified you;
I ordained you a prophet to the nations.
— JEREMIAH 1:5

God then unfolded to Jeremiah what this would mean to him, and the stewardship of this knowledge radically affected the rest of his life.

Another helpful example of this truth is found in the witness of the apostle Paul as he related what God had told him: "God . . . from my mother's womb set me apart and called me by His grace" (Galatians 1:15 NIV). Much of the Book of Acts is the record of what this call of God meant for Paul's life. Such love of God, Paul said, literally "constrained" him ("constrained" means to order all of the rest of his life). In this special relationship with God, he increasingly became convinced that, "He died for all so that those who live should no longer live for themselves, but for the One who died for them and was raised" (2 Corinthians 5:15 HCSB). Paul went on later to express what this meant in his life in saying, "But by God's grace I am what I am, and His grace toward me was not ineffective. However, I worked more than any of them, yet not I, but God's grace that was with me"

(1 Corinthians 15:10 HCSB), thus express-
ing his enormous sense of accountability to
God for such love toward him.

But this sense of call and accountability
was not limited in the New Testament to just
a few special people. **Every** believer is spoken of as the "called of God," or the "chosen
of God," or "ones set apart by God"! (You
may want to look up this fact in the following passages: Romans 1:6; 1 Corinthians
1:1–2; Ephesians 1:1–6, 18; Ephesians 4:1;
1 Thessalonians 1:4; 2 Thessalonians 1:11.)

No one can adequately come to the knowledge of God's truth, for themselves or for
others, without a thorough commitment
to the place and authority of God's Word
(both the Old and New Testament). It is in
the Scriptures that God has chosen to reveal Himself and His will for our lives. As
a person approaches the Bible and opens its
pages, he or she comes face-to-face with the
Author — God! The Holy Spirit is present
to open the mind and heart of the child of
God to an immediate Word from God for his
or her life (John 14:16–17; John 16:13–15; 1
Corinthians 2:10–16). Without this commitment to encounter God in His Word, one is
left to human reasoning alone — something
that will never lead to God or an understanding of His Word. This entire study is

based on the assumption that the reader is committed to meet God in His Word and in turn respond to Him in this encounter.

As the Scriptures are our guide for both faith and practice, or daily living, this truth and its implications for each of our lives will guide us thoroughly in our relationship with God. This study will help us understand and respond to God in accountability. In this pursuit, we will look at:

1. **Who** are the called?
2. **Why** does God call us?
3. **What** is a call?
4. **How** am I called?
5. **When** am I called?
6. **How** do I live out the call?

UNIT ONE
WHO ARE THE CALLED?

MEMORY VERSE FOR THE WEEK

The eyes of the Lord run to and fro throughout the whole earth, to show Himself strong on behalf of those whose heart is loyal to Him. 2 CHRONICLES 16:9

ESSENTIAL TRUTH FOR THE WEEK

Every believer is called to "walk worthy of the calling with which you were called." EPHESIANS 4:1–3

I, therefore, the prisoner of the Lord, beseech you to walk worthy of the calling with which you were called, with all lowliness and gentleness, with longsuffering, bearing with one another in love, endeavoring to keep the unity of the Spirit with the bond of peace." EPHESIANS 4:1–3

RON AND ANGELA WILSON

Martial Arts from God's Perspective

I received a call from Ron requesting that we get together to meet. Ron and his family had recently begun attending the church I was pastoring. Sensing a call to ministry, Ron had sold his business in the northeast and had moved to Little Rock to work with a ministry. He was frustrated at this ministry, as he was spending his time on a computer filling out reports and feeling out of place and overwhelmed with the confines of his cubical. You see, Ron had run a successful martial arts club and was a Master in Wing Chung Kung Fu. He had never worked with computers or functioned in an office. For reasons unclear, the ministry he had contacted when he felt called to ministry had counseled him to sell his Kung Fu studio, move across the country, and sit at a desk so that he could "minister."

Ron loved people and loved to share the gospel, he just didn't love the computer or his cubical. I remember the sense of wonder

I had as this gifted man who had studied his martial arts for over 30 years had sold all of his equipment and studio so that he could be "in ministry." Ron is a man who has never met a stranger and can immediately meet people and build relationships. Over the next months, I helped Ron see that he was indeed called to ministry, but this did not mean he had to dismiss all that God had done in his life for the past 30 years. Ron quickly left this ministry he had moved his family to join and came on staff at our church as the evangelism minister. He started a free Kung Fu and Tai Chi ministry for the community and began going door to door sharing the gospel and inviting people to the church to learn martial arts.

Because of Ron's skills in martial arts, people quickly began to come to church to study. During the break time, Ron would share a short Bible study and invite the class to church. He tied his martial arts to biblical truths and required Scripture memory in order to advance in belts or rank. In addition to mastering the martial arts skills to advance to the first belt, Ron required that the students memorized the "Romans Road" Scriptures. It was a regular occurrence for Ron to share about who had come to a saving faith in Christ from his classes.

Today Ron is back in the Northeast using

his martial arts to minister in church planting and prison ministry. He was called to ministry, but God did not intend to waste all the years Ron had invested in his training and business so that he could sit at a computer, God simply wanted to reorientate Ron and his wife, Angela, to take their gifts and talents for His kingdom purposes. When you understand that you are called by God, it may simply be that God wants you to take your training, experience, and the things you love and use them to serve Him in our world.

DAY 1
ALL ARE CALLED

You may be asking, "But just who are the called? Are they a special group of persons? What about my life? Am I called too? How would I know? What would it look like?"

And sincerely your heart may be saying, "Lord, I do love You! I do belong to You! I am Your servant, and I truly want to serve You. But Lord, am I really called to be on mission with You in my world? Lord, just who are the called?"

⊸⎯⎯⎯⎯⊷

Unfortunately, as we have made a difference between clergy and laypeople, so we have made a difference between the specially called and the common believer. All are called!

⊸⎯⎯⎯⎯⊷

Unfortunately, our "Christian culture" has

26

not always been thoroughly biblical. That is, we have made such a difference between clergy and nonclergy in the church that we have created two classes of "called." All are called! The difference is not whether we are called or not, but in the nature of the assignment given by God. But every believer is one who is called by God, for Him to be free to accomplish His purposes in them and through them!

Let's look briefly at some Scripture passages that assure us that every believer is called. In Exodus 19, when God created a special nation through whom He would bring salvation to the whole world, He said:

> *"You have seen what I did to the Egyptians, and how I bore you on eagles' wings and brought you to Myself. Now therefore, if you will indeed obey My voice and keep My covenant, then you shall be a special treasure to Me above all people; for all the earth is Mine. And you shall be to Me a kingdom of priests and a holy nation." These are the words which you shall speak to the children of Israel. EXODUS 19:4–6*

He said they would be a kingdom of priests — not a kingdom with a priesthood. Each and every one of them would be priests unto

God. The Levites would be the ones assigned to train and equip the entire nation to walk with God as priests unto God so He could fulfill His purposes to save the nations of the world through them. This same truth is stated in the New Testament.

> *You also, as living stones, are being built up a spiritual house, a holy priesthood, to offer up spiritual sacrifices acceptable to God through Jesus Christ. . . . But you are a chosen generation, a royal priesthood, a holy nation, His own special people, that you may proclaim the praises of Him who called you out of darkness into His marvelous light; who once were not a people but are now the people of God, who had not obtained mercy but now have obtained mercy.* 1 PETER 2:5, 9–10

Notice how Paul addressed the people of the church at Rome. *Through Him we have received grace and apostleship for obedience to the faith among all nations for His name, among whom you also are the called of Jesus Christ.* ROMANS 1:5–6

What does Paul say he received grace and apostleship for?

Yes, it was for obedience to the faith. There is little question that those who receive salvation from God have at the same time released themselves to obey the call that comes from faith. They go hand in hand.

When you received Christ into your life, did you understand that at that same moment you were releasing your life to be used anyway that God would choose?
❏ Yes
❏ No
❏ Maybe

As you have lived out your Christian life, describe how you have released your life to God for Him to use to accomplish His purposes. What adjustments did you make as you responded to God's plan in obedience?

_____

_____

_____

_____

If you aren't making adjustments, you are in a dangerous place. Each believer is called of God and is to function before God and a watching world as a priest unto God. God, therefore, promised that He would enable every believer to function this way by the empowering presence of His Holy Spirit.

Read 1 Corinthians 2:10–13. What does the Holy Spirit know about the things of God?

_____

_____

_____

_____

According to verse 12, why have Christians been given the Holy Spirit?

_____

_____

_____

_____

God eternally planned that every believer would be spiritually equipped to both know and do the will of God, as He would reveal it to each one.

———❧———

The Holy Spirit has been given so that we can know what has been freely given to us by God. As you live out the call of God on your life, the heavenly Father will shape your life and provide all you need to follow Him. As He provides for your life, the Holy Spirit has been assigned to help you recognize and experience all the provision of God for your life.

Read 1 Corinthians 1:26–31 and answer the following questions.

According to these verses, what are the qualifications to be called of God?

_____

_____

_____

_____

Why does God choose/call the foolish, weak, base, and despised things to use as His instruments?

_____

_____

_____

_____

Have you ever excluded yourself from service to God because you did not feel qualified? Based on this passage, do you think that God could and does desire to use your life in His kingdom?

_____

_____

_____

_____

THOUGHT FOR THE DAY

There is no separation or distinction in the call of God between those recognized as leaders and other Christians; all Christians are called to a saving faith, and in this call, all must release their lives to God for His purposes.

Day 2
Completeness of His Call

Have you noticed the completeness of God's call and equipping of all people — sons, daughters, men, and women? This includes your life too!

It is interesting and encouraging to realize that throughout the Bible, most of the people God called and worked through mightily are what we today would call *everyday* believers. They were very ordinary people, called and enabled by God, to work with Him in their world. Their abilities or skills were not as important as their relationship with God. Their heart relationship of love and trust in God always determined how much God was able to do through them.

⚊⚋⚊

Their abilities or skills were not as important as their relationship with God.

He also chose David His servant, and took him from the sheepfolds; from following the ewes that had young He brought him, to shepherd Jacob His people, and Israel His inheritance. So he shepherded them according to the integrity of his heart, and guided them by the skillfulness of his hands. PSALM 78:70–72

David was a shepherd (see Psalm 78:70–72), and God chose him for a special assignment, in which God would guide His people through him. According to Scripture, Amos said he was:

No prophet, nor was I a son of a prophet, but I was a sheepbreeder and a tender of sycamore fruit. Then the Lord took me as I followed the flock, and the Lord said to me, "Go, prophesy to My people Israel." AMOS 7:14–15

Peter was a fisherman, and all the other disciples were what we would call "just ordinary people" — until God assigned them roles in His kingdom where He would work through them mightily to accomplish His purposes. This has continued to be God's way to this very day.

Let's take a look at some ordinary people that God called and used in extravagant ways from the Scriptures.

Read Joshua 2:1–14. In verse 1, how does the Bible describe Rahab?

_____

_____

_____

_____

How did God use Rahab (the harlot) to accomplish His purposes for Israel?

_____

_____

_____

_____

Rahab and her whole family were saved when God gave the city of Jericho to Israel. She was an ordinary person who recognized God's activity in His people (vv. 9–11), and God used her life in extraordinary ways. Notice that Rahab is listed in Matthew 1:5 as the mother of Boaz in the genealogy of Jesus. She is also described in Hebrews 11:31 and James 2:25 as a woman of faith.

Read Colossians 4:14. How does Colossians 4:14 describe Luke?

_____

_____

_____

_____

Luke was a physician who accompanied Paul in his tour of Asia and Macedonia (see also Acts 16:10–13, 20:5–6; to Jerusalem, Acts 21:1–18; to Rome, Acts 27, 28; 2 Timothy 4:11; Philemon 24). It is also very important to note that when we look at the New Testament, Luke wrote more of it than any other person as God inspired him to write the Gospel of Luke and the Book of Acts. God called a doctor and made him a disciple and called him into service. When you read about all that happened to Paul, can you see why God would place a doctor with him on his travels? (See 2 Corinthians 11:23–29.)

How ordinary is your life compared to God's special assignment for you? Remember the Scripture from Day One of this week (1 Corinthians 1:26–31). He chooses the ordinary and the ones that the world would not choose so that when He has completed His work, He alone will receive the glory.

The key is not our talents, but the cultivating of our heart so that when God does work through us, we can turn and praise Him and let others know that it was God who accomplished the work.

———

The key is not our talents, but the cultivating of our heart so that when God does work through us we can turn and praise Him and let others know that it was God who accomplished the work.

———

Today we have seen how God called a:

- shepherd to be a king
- sheepbreeder to be a prophet
- fisherman to be one of the 12 disciples
- prostitute to be an instrument of protection for God's people
- doctor to be a companion of the Apostle Paul and the author of two New Testament books (Luke and Acts)

What about you? Is your heart ready for God to use you in any way He chooses?

Spend some time praying today that God would open your eyes, ears, and heart so that you clearly recognize His voice when He calls. We will see tomorrow the process God uses to equip those He calls.

THOUGHT FOR THE DAY

No believer should let fear of failure prevent them from responding fully to the call of God. Everything needed for life and godliness has been provided and is immediately at work in every life that obeys God's call.

REVIEW YOUR MEMORY VERSE
FOR THE WEEK.

The _____ *of the Lord run to and fro throughout the whole earth, to show Himself* _____ *on behalf of those whose* _____ *is loyal to Him.* 2 CHRONICLES 16:9

DAY 3
JESUS EQUIPS THE CALLED

You may be thinking that you are not equipped to do this. In John 17, Jesus revealed to us that the Father gives our lives to Jesus for Him to develop and teach us. For what purpose? To make us useful vessels that His Father can use to save a lost and dying world. In His significant prayer, Jesus said to the Father:

I have glorified You on the earth. I have finished the work which You have given Me to do. . . . I have manifested Your name to the men whom You have given Me out of the world. They were Yours, You gave them to Me, and they have kept Your word. Now they have known that all things which You have given Me are from You For I have given to them the words which You have given Me; and they have received them, and have known surely that I came forth from You; and they have believed that You sent Me. . . . And the glory which You gave Me I have given them, that they may be one just as We are one: I in them, and You in Me; that they may be made perfect in one, and that the world may know that You have sent Me, and have loved them as You have loved Me. JOHN 17:4, 6–8, 22–23

When Jesus called the first disciples, He assured them of His responsibility for their lives: *"Then Jesus said to them 'Follow Me, and I will make you become fishers of men.'"* MARK 1:17

Whose responsibility was it for the disciples to become fishers of men?
❑ Jesus
❑ Disciples

Jesus would be the one who, under the instruction of the Father, would teach the disciples of the kingdom of God that they would soon give their lives as fishers of men. The disciples were simply responsible to stay with Jesus to learn and practice what He taught.

This is the will of the Father who sent Me, that of all He has given Me I should lose nothing, but should raise it up at the last day. JOHN 6:39

All of the Gospels record how Jesus taught, trained, guided, encouraged, empowered, and fully equipped His disciples for all the Father had in mind to do through them. How has Jesus been equipping you for all that the heavenly Father has in mind for you?

Look over the past year and write down specific ways that Jesus, through the Holy Spirit, has been equipping you. How has He trained you:

_____

_____

_____

_____

guided you:

_____

_____

_____

_____

encouraged you:

_____

_____

_____

_____

empowered you:

_____

_____

_____

_____

John 17 reveals just how thoroughly Jesus prepared them for their mission in their world. Your life and mine are included in that very prayer in John 17.

———◦———

Our living Lord has accepted your life from the Father and is at work "making you to become" all God wants you to be.

———◦———

As Jesus said, "I do not pray for these alone, but also for those who will believe in Me through their word" (John 17:20). So you need not be concerned that you are not fully prepared to be of use to God.

THOUGHT FOR THE DAY

Our living Lord has accepted your life from the Father and is at work "making you to become" all God wants you to be.

Spend the rest of your time today praying. Thank God for all of the times He trained you, guided you, encouraged you, and empowered you. Be specific in your prayer and don't be surprised if the Holy Spirit reveals even more of the Father's activity to you as you spend time praising and thanking Him.

DAY 4
YOU ARE IMPORTANT TO GOD!

Each one of us is important to God! We are ordinary people who love God with all our hearts, and who know that the call to salvation is also a call to be laborers together with God in our world. As we respond to the call of God and yield to Him, He powerfully accomplishes His purpose to save a lost world through our lives. God seeks out those who are willing to "stand before Him on behalf of the land."

<hr />

God seeks out those who are willing to "stand before Him on behalf of the land."

<hr />

"So I sought for a man among them who would make a wall, and stand in the gap before Me on behalf of the land, that I

*should not destroy it; but I found no one.
Therefore I have poured out My indignation
on them; I have consumed them with the
fire of my wrath; and I have recompensed
their deeds on their own heads," says the
Lord God.* EZEKIEL 22:30–31

If He cannot find a person to "stand in the
gap," the land and the people are destroyed.
But when He does find someone who is willing to be used, He is able to save multitudes
of people.

When Jonah finally obeyed God's assignment to take His message to the people of
the great city of Nineveh, the king and all
the people responded with immediate and
thorough repentance, and the entire city
was saved. This was the heart of God, and it
waited on the obedience of an ordinary child
of God. We may not understand why God
chooses to use individuals and often waits on
their response before He responds, but that
He chooses to work through people is clear.
If we have been unwilling to be "the one"
that God could use as His instrument, then
we must ask ourselves, "What could have
been if only I had responded immediately to
God's invitation to join Him for the lost?"
We can get caught up in our own world and
not recognize that there are people whose

lives hang in the balance as God waits on our response to Him.

And Mordecai told them to answer Esther: "Do not think in your heart that you will escape in the king's palace any more than all the other Jews. For if you remain completely silent at this time, relief and deliverance will arise for the Jews from another place, but you and your father's house will perish. Yet who knows whether you have come to the kingdom for such a time as this?" ESTHER 4:13–14

Esther was a very ordinary woman. But she had "come to the kingdom for such a time as this" (Esther 4:13–14). Her response was vital to the heart of God for His people. Their lives and destiny hung in the balance. She literally risked her life, but God worked through her to save His people, and we know of her life and deeds to this very day.

Many other women were just as vital. Hannah brought forth the great prophet, priest, and judge, Samuel. Deborah saved God's people from their enemy (Judges 4,

5). Elizabeth and Mary were available to God for the bringing of John the Baptist and Jesus. And Mary Magdalene was greatly used of God, one day at a time, to minister to Jesus and His disciples, and was therefore greatly honored of God.

Can you call to the Lord and say to Him what Isaiah said?

> Also I heard the voice of the Lord, saying: "Whom shall I send, and who will go for Us?" Then I said, "Here am I! Send me."
> ISAIAH 6:8

Often people look at Isaiah's response and feel that it is only for "sending me" to a great task. However, God is looking over your home, church, community, city, and beyond when He asks *whom shall I send? Whom shall I send* into the schools or the soccer and football fields? *Whom shall I send* into the community center, the hospitals, and the business places?

We need to be reminded of another Scripture that reads:

> The eyes of the Lord run to and fro throughout the whole earth, to show Him-

47

self strong on behalf of those whose heart is loyal to Him. 2 CHRONICLES 16:9

What is God looking over the earth to do, according to this passage?

_____

_____

_____

_____

_____

Does this surprise you that God is looking for someone to use and work through to display His strength to a watching world? What do you think the Lord sees when He looks at your life?

_____

_____

_____

_____

_____

_____

Could He describe your heart as being loyal to Him? Do your attitudes, thoughts, and actions reveal a heart that is loyal to Him?

_____

_____

_____

_____

THOUGHT FOR THE DAY

You can never fully estimate the value of your life to God. To God, eternity is always at stake! Your obedience releases the fullness of God in accomplishing His purpose to redeem a lost world and even to inaugurate eternity in His fullness of time.

Do you sense that God is looking over your life and asking you to go with Him to touch your world? Do you know of some areas that He has been asking you to serve but you have not yet responded? How is He sending you, as a child of God, to be involved in His work?

_____

_____

_____

REVIEW YOUR MEMORY VERSE
FOR THE WEEK.

The _____ *of the Lord run*
_____ _____ _____
throughout the whole earth, to show Himself
_____ *on behalf of those whose*
_____ *is* _____ *to Him.*
2 CHRONICLES 16:9

DAY 5
TAKING A SPIRITUAL INVENTORY

Now is an appropriate time to do what we call "taking a spiritual inventory"! The inventory is found on pages 54–56, and you'll be asked to complete it at the end of today's study. In light of all the Scriptures you have studied, with the Holy Spirit as your teacher, the inventory will help you evaluate how you are doing.

Such an inventory is necessary for every sincere believer! Too often Christians want to have, for example, the "faith of Abraham," but, they do not realize that it took God about 40 years to develop Abraham's character to the point where he would immediately respond to God's commands. During those years of development, God often reviewed His covenant with Abraham, found in Genesis 12:1–4. He also brought Moses constantly before Him to remind him of Moses' walk with God. He did this with David as well, and in Psalm 51 we see

51

the major changes David had to make to "restore to [him] the joy of His salvation" (v. 12). And Jesus had to take His disciples aside constantly to explain how their continuing lack of faith was affecting their relationship with Him.

God must take each of us aside regularly, remind us of His call in our life, bring to our remembrance all He has said to us (John 14:26), and help us see how we are responding to His shaping and guiding of our lives.

—✦—

To Him alone are we accountable. Therefore, it is before Him and in His presence that we must stand for a spiritual evaluation — done by God.

—✦—

A spiritual inventory must be done in the presence of God! He alone has lordship in our lives. To Him alone are we accountable. Therefore, it is before Him and in His presence that we must stand for a spiritual evaluation — done by God. You may sense that He is saying, "Well done, good and faithful servant. You have been faithful in a little, I can now give you more!" Or you may sense

God is grieved, and is exclaiming, "Why do you keep calling Me 'Lord! Lord!' yet never do anything that I say?"

Paul assured believers that they could stand face-to-face with God, with "no veil" in between them and God. But he said that when they stood face-to-face with God they would be "transformed into the same image from glory to glory" (2 Corinthians 3:18). When a believer is face-to-face with God, there is an automatic "inventory" taken by God — Christlikeness! When we stand before God we become very aware of our own lives. Do you remember Peter's response when He met the Lord in his fishing boat in Luke 5? "Depart from me, for I am a sinful man" (Luke 5:8). Isaiah had a similar response when he met God in the Temple as he stated, "Woe is me, for I am undone! Because I am a man of unclean lips, and I dwell in the midst of a people of unclean lips; for my eyes have seen the King, the Lord of hosts" (Isaiah 6:5). Both of these men ultimately were used of God, but when they met the Lord they saw themselves as God saw them and they submitted their lives to God.

This standing before God comes when we, with transparent honesty, bring ourselves before God and allow Him to cleanse our lives by the "washing of water by the word"

(Ephesians 5:26–27). The regular reading and study of God's Word is a must for every believer.

Prayer also brings us into God's presence, where God changes our ways into His ways and we cry out as Jesus did, "Not my will, but Thine be done!"

In summary, here are the important ingredients of a "spiritual inventory":

1. Do it before God.
2. Do it with His Word and with prayer as your standard.
3. Do it with transparent honesty.
4. Do it thoroughly.
5. Ask the right questions:

❑ Am I a believer?
❑ Do I therefore know that I am called by God?
❑ Does this include being on mission with God?
❑ Does my life give constant evidence that I have released my life fully to Him?

THOUGHT FOR THE DAY

A spiritual inventory must be done in the presence of God. It is God alone to whom we are accountable. Take time now to fill out your spiritual inventory on pages 57–59.

What do these inventory questions reveal to you?

_____

_____

_____

_____

_____

_____

REVIEWING WEEK ONE

Look back over this week's lesson. Pray and ask God to reveal one (or more) statements or Scriptures that He wants you to understand, learn, or practice. **Write it on the lines below.**

_____

_____

_____

_____

Reword the statement or Scripture into a prayer of response to God.

_____

_____

_____

_____

What does God want you to do in response to this week's study? (Take a moment to record this on the "Final Thoughts Summary" found on p. 284–285.)

_____

_____

_____

_____

Review this week's memory verse. Turn it into a prayer of response to God. For example, *"Dear Lord, I know You are looking throughout the whole earth to show Yourself strong on behalf of those whose heart is loyal to You. I want to be used by You in my generation. Please show me if there are any areas in my life where my heart is not completely loyal to You. Give me wisdom and courage to make the necessary changes so that You can fully use my life to touch a hurting world. Amen."*

_____

_____

_____

_____

MY SPIRITUAL INVENTORY

Date: _____

As you consider your life, list key events in which God has clearly directed you.

_____

_____

_____

_____

_____

_____

_____

_____

Now, as you look back over the last year, can you see areas in which God has been working in your life?

_____

_____

_____

_____

_____

_____

_____

_____

As you reflect on God's activity in your life, list adjustments you have made in order to join Him in His activity.

_____

_____

_____

_____

_____

_____

Should the Holy Spirit remind you of some "unfinished" business (something you have known that God wanted you to do, but you never adjusted your life to obey), write it below and make a commitment to quickly adjust your life so that you can obey in this area.

_____

_____

_____

_____

_____

_____

_____

Take time to ask the Lord to show you
what He thinks of your life and of your
obedience to Him. What is His response? Be ready to make adjustments
in your life in order to respond to His
perspective of your life.

_____

_____

_____

_____

_____

_____

ARTHUR AND MARION CLARK

AN ORDINARY COUPLE WHO AFFECTED ETERNITY

Arthur served in the business world as an accountant all his life. He was a faithful deacon in our church, serving wherever he was asked. Marion was committed to prayer and to missions. Under the preaching of God's Word, they both felt God had something more for their lives. They felt led to be available to God and to their church by being a lay-pastor/wife team in an attempted church plant in the Russian community just north of our city. The church saw their lives and affirmed their sense of call — ordinary people, but now called of God to serve in church planting. They served in this community for six years, leading many children, some youth, and several adults to the Lord. However, this community was a very "closed" community, and not one person came for baptism, or to join the new work. Arthur and Marion were often disheartened. This was their first experience in church planting. Both myself, as their pastor, and the entire church saw their devotion to the Lord, and affirmed them. Arthur even taught accounting at our theological college. Arthur was diagnosed with cancer and eventually died. But the influence of their lives affected their daughter and her husband, who then pastored faithfully for many years. Now Arthur and Marion's grandson is pastoring in Arkansas, and is a highly respected pastor.

An ordinary couple clearly sensing God's call, and responding with a sacred accountability to that call, affected eternity for many who would not otherwise have known the Savior, and in turn affected their own family to two generations. While they may have not seen all the visible fruit in the church plant where they served, there was fruit indeed. Their faithfulness was an inspiration to countless church members who were in turn called to ministry in various ways. Arthur's willingness to serve in the college touched the lives of many, and generations of Arthur and Marion's own family were impacted by the spiritual heritage they created. Their service will be rewarded in heaven.

UNIT TWO
WHY DOES
GOD CALL US?

MEMORY VERSE FOR THE WEEK

And whatever you do, do it heartily, as to the Lord and not to men, knowing that from the Lord you will receive the reward of the inheritance; for you serve the Lord Christ. COLOSSIANS 3:23–24

ESSENTIAL TRUTH FOR THE WEEK

The entire Bible bears witness to the truth that God, from eternity, chose to work through His people to accomplish His eternal purposes in the world. He could have worked everything by Himself, just as He worked in creation, but He chose not to do it that way. Rather, the Bible tells how God called individuals into a special relationship with Himself so that He could use them to accomplish His purposes.

G. R. S. BLACKABY:
AN ORDINARY BUSINESSMAN

TESTIMONY FROM HENRY BLACKABY ABOUT HIS FATHER

I knew my dad as a very ordinary businessman who was a committed Christian in his workplace. He was born in England and immigrated to Canada as a young man, seeking adventure in Canada. He began to work for the Bank of Montreal and soon became a branch manager. He was moved regularly, but he always sought to be an open Christian wherever he was placed. Early in his life he knew that God had a special place for him — where and how he did not know. But that he would be faithful to His Lord was obvious. As I was growing up I watched him witness to all who came into his life. He was, to me, the greatest soul-winner I have ever known: to the down and out, to the businessmen with whom he worked, and to anyone he came into contact within the city where he lived. Because of his faithful witness and conscientious walk with God, he was recognized as a Christian with integrity at every city or town where he lived.

Dad was always bringing people into our home. As he would enter, he would ask us to pray for him and this person because he was going to share with them about the Lord. He would then appear in the doorway a little while later and say that his guest had something he wanted to say. We had come to know that through the tears someone would tell us that he had received Christ into his life and we would rejoice together.

My father, who was a deacon, believed that every deacon should preach, teach, lead others in prayer, and begin a church if there was not one available. He started a church in a dance hall and preached every Sunday until (after several years) we finally got a pastor. He was an ordinary man, a businessman, who let God use him in countless ways to make Christ known. After his death, my brothers and I had many people come up to us and say, "Your dad was the finest Christian I ever knew. He made a loan to me — on character and with prayer. He was the only one who believed in me, and I am what I am today because of your godly father." What a heritage we have because of my dad's faithfulness.

Our home was a place of prayer for all peoples. This was especially true of the First Nations (Native Americans in the United States) believers from the surrounding reserves. On *our knees we prayed for a mighty move of God among these dear people. My own sense of call into the ministry, and my life commitment to the native peoples, came from my godly father's influence. I saw that an ordinary child of God could be greatly used of God — unnoticed by much of the world, but known in heaven. Many children, youth, and adults will be in heaven for eternity because of the faithful witness of my father, an ordinary businessman who had discovered his place in God's eternal purposes.*

Day 1
God's Word Reveals God and His Ways

When God was about to destroy every living thing from the earth because of sin, He called Noah to Himself, and through Noah, preserved his family and enough living creatures to begin to populate the earth again (Genesis 6–10). When God wanted to begin the process of shaping a nation to bring salvation to mankind He chose Abraham. He used Abraham to be the father of Israel as well as an example of faith to the end of time (Genesis 12–22; Hebrews 11:8). When God was ready to deliver His chosen people from bondage in Egypt, He called Moses to Himself and sent him to be the one through whom He would accomplish this task (Exodus 3).

God called individuals into a special relationship with Himself to use them to accomplish His purposes.

The entire Bible bears witness to the truth that God, from eternity, chose to work through His people to accomplish His eternal purposes in the world. He could have worked everything by Himself, just as He worked in creation, but He chose not to do it that way. Rather, the Bible tells how God called individuals into a special relationship with Himself so that He could use them to accomplish His purposes.

The fact that God chooses to use people to accomplish His purposes can be seen throughout the entire Bible. It is still His way to this very hour. God calls individuals He can trust to be the instruments through which He will accomplish His eternal purposes, especially His purpose to save those who are lost.

The Example of Mary

One of the most significant illustrations of hearing and responding to God is found in the life of Mary, Jesus' mother. God's eternal purpose was to bring a Savior into the world, and through that Savior to bring His great salvation to every person. He found the one through whom He would choose to work — Mary, a servant girl. An angel from God announced God's purpose through her. Then came her amazing and wonderful response: "'Behold the maidservant of the Lord! Let it be to me according to your word.' And the angel departed from her" (Luke 1:38). And God did what He said He would do! Impossible to man, but possible with God (Luke 1:37). Mary had a heart that was "perfect toward God" and God "showed Himself strong" on her behalf (2 Chronicles 16:9). This has been God's strategy from eternity, and still is — with each of us today.

What are some things you can "build" into your life so that you are ready when God invites you to join Him in His work? Check all that apply.
❑ Daily Bible study
❑ Daily prayertime
❑ Fellowship with other believers
❑ Being a part of a local church
❑ Accountability to other believers

We will see over the next few weeks that much of how God can or chooses to use us is dependent on our willingness to get to know Him and how prepared we are to let Him shape our lives. It may seem simplistic, but the most basic way this happens is through regular Bible study, prayer, and worship.

Do you think God wants to use your life to accomplish His eternal purposes?
❏ Yes
❏ No
❏ I don't know

Of course, God wants to use your life to accomplish His eternal purpose in this generation! However, there are times when God looks for someone to use, but does not find anyone who is willing or living in a way that God could trust them with His work. When God does not have someone who will allow their life to be used, it will often have serious consequences. One well-known example of this is found in Ezekiel:

> *"So I sought for a man among them who would make a wall, and stand in the gap before Me on behalf of the land, that I should not destroy it; but I found no one. Therefore I have poured out My indignation on them; I have consumed them with the fire of My wrath; and I have recompensed their deeds on their own heads," says the Lord God.* EZEKIEL 22:30–31

This is a most sobering truth, revealed by God — to us — so each of us must take seriously any invitation of God. This may be to share about God's love to our family or our neighbors, or to take part in a missions project. It may be joining a committee at your child's school, reaching out to a co-worker, or even changing careers. The eternal destiny of others may rest in our response to His invitation and call. And the Bible makes it clear that He will hold us accountable for our response.

—⁌⁍—

The eternal destiny of others may rest in our response to God's invitation and call. He will also hold us accountable for our response to His invitation.

—⁌⁍—

God does not want His people to suffer judgment, but rather wants people to honor Him and receive His blessing. In Ezekiel's day, God appointed him to warn the people of the pending danger of rebelling against God. In this assignment, God called Ezekiel a "watchman" for God's people. God described the awesome responsibility of a watchman in Ezekiel 33:1–20. Once Ezekiel had God's message for His people, he was accountable for delivering it. This same truth applies to every Christian today. God has placed His people as watchmen and watchwomen in family life, the workplace, the church, and neighborhoods. Their purpose is clear: to share the good news of God's word as well as to share the danger of rejecting God's invitation to salvation. Every Christian must recognize the serious accountability presented in Ezekiel 33:1–20 and apply it to their own lives today. This is why it is imperative that we believe the Scriptures. They reveal God and His ways, so that when God approaches us we will know that it is God, know how to respond to God, and know the serious nature of the consequences — for good and for bad.

Read Ezekiel 33:1–20 to see the awesome message and accountability God assigned to Ezekiel.

Where has God placed you as a watchperson?

_____

_____

_____

_____

Has God placed a burden on your heart for those around you? If so, are you praying for these people daily?

_____

_____

_____

Can you see how God has placed you as a watchperson in your home or workplace?

_____

_____

_____

—◦◦◦—

The Scriptures reveal God and His ways, so that when God approaches us we will know that it is God and know how to respond to Him.

—◦◦◦—

You may be thinking that this example from the life of Ezekiel is a little extreme compared to your life. But if you think about it, do you know someone who is making choices that will lead them away from Christ? What is their ultimate end if they do not have

74

a personal relationship with Jesus Christ? There may be someone at work or in your neighborhood about to do something that will put their marriage in jeopardy, impacting the future of their entire family. It is imperative to recognize when God is inviting you to be a watchperson. He may ask you to warn a loved one, to intercede for a friend, to encourage a colleague to turn to God, or to speak to a family member about honoring God in their marriage.

Let me share an example of this truth from the life of my wife, Dana. She currently works in the field of education in the public schools. At one point, she was working next door to a Christian teacher whose heart was set on divorcing her husband. As Dana observed the situation each day, she became convinced that the only way to help this family was through intercession. She began praying daily for the co-worker, her husband, and their children. She also enlisted others to pray at our church. Day after day, she prayed consistently for the co-worker. One particular weekend, Dana was sick with a virus. As she rested in bed, she continued in prayer for this family throughout the weekend. On Monday, when she went back to work, the woman was a different person. She was smiling, happy, and telling co-workers that she and her husband had reconciled over the weekend. What a miracle! Often, we want to council co-workers or share Scriptures with them in order to help them through a difficult situation. However, there are times when the only access you will have to a friend or co-worker is through prayer. But, don't ever forget, prayer is one of the greatest ways that we can serve as a watch-person in our workplace, neighborhood, or family!

As you begin to see yourself as a watch-person — pray daily for those God has put around you. Ask God to give you His perspective as you interact with those He as placed in your life. As you pray for these people, God will give you insights into their lives. The way you view them will change. Instead of avoiding someone who isn't like you — you will begin to see the pain in their life and, in turn, have a desire to carry their burdens.

For the eyes of the Lord run to and fro throughout the whole earth, to show Himself strong on behalf of those whose heart is loyal to Him.
2 CHRONICLES 16:9

Behold, I am the Lord, the God of all flesh. Is anything too hard for Me? JEREMIAH 32:27

❦

Maybe you are recognizing that you have not been a faithful watchperson where God has placed you. Stop and spend time asking God to forgive you and release your life to be used by Him for His purposes today.

Ask God to show you people He has placed in your life who desperately need to have a relationship with Him. Or, maybe He will reveal someone who has turned away from following God and needs to return to Him. Write the names of those God brings to your mind on the following lines and record their names in your prayer journal. Make this a matter of prayer this week and watch to see what happens next.

_____

_____

_____

_____

THOUGHT FOR THE DAY

God chooses to work through His people to accomplish His eternal purpose. He desires

77

to use each of His children as watchmen in their families, workplaces, communities, and throughout the world.

Have you arranged your life to be ready when God comes to you? Are you watching and available to Him? If you would have to say, "No, my life is not really in order to be used," then take time now and ask God to show you what changes you need to make so that you are available for His service.

_____

_____

_____

_____

DAY 2
CALLED: NOT FOR TIME, BUT ETERNITY

In understanding the call of God in our lives, it is important to realize that God did not make us for time, but for eternity. We were created in His image (Genesis 1:26–27). This includes immortality (living for eternity). Jesus Himself declared constantly that the ones who believe in Him will have eternal life: "Whoever believes in Him should not perish but have eternal life" (JOHN 3:15).

———

Then God said, "Let Us make man in Our image, according to Our likeness. . . ." So God created man in His own image; in the image of God He created him; male and female He created them. GENESIS 1:26–27

My sheep hear My voice, and I know them, and they follow Me. And I give them eternal life, and they shall never perish; neither shall anyone snatch them out of My hand. JOHN 10:27–28

Paul also charged Timothy to lay hold of eternal life:

"Fight the good fight of faith, lay hold of eternal life, to which you were also called and have confessed the good confession in the presence of many witnesses." 1 TIMOTHY 6:12

Thus, God's goal is not time, but eternity. This life, then, is to prepare us for eternity. This was God's purpose from before the foundation of the world. Jesus further urged His disciples, "Do not lay up for yourselves treasures on earth . . . but lay up for yourselves treasures in heaven" (Matthew 6:19–20).

What are some things that would be considered "eternal things" or "treasures in heaven"?
❑ Time invested in people
❑ Intercession
❑ Teaching your children God's ways
❑ Volunteering in disaster-relief efforts

- ❑ Caring for widows, orphans, or home-bound
- ❑ Investing financially in organizations that minister to people

- ❑ _____
- ❑ _____
- ❑ _____
- ❑ _____

What are some things that would be considered "perishable things" or "treasures on earth"?

- ❑ Sole focus on climbing the corporate ladder
- ❑ Investing time on your golf game when your neighbor is lost or hurting
- ❑ Growing wealth
- ❑ Hobbies, collections, awards

- ❑ _____
- ❑ _____
- ❑ _____

Looking at the two lists that you have made, where have you been investing your time and energy . . . on eternal pursuits or worldly pursuits?

_____

The time that we have should be spent with "eternal investments" in the forefront of our heart and mind. This is why Paul stated:

And whatever you do, do it heartily, as to the Lord and not to men, knowing that from the Lord you will receive the reward of the inheritance; for you serve the Lord Christ. COLOSSIANS 3:23–24

Such incredible truth causes the Christian to pursue eternity, using "time" as God's gift in this pursuit. Therefore, every Christian must seek to use the whole of his or her time, to fulfill the call God has place on their life. God's call is His invitation to invest in eternity by making our lives available to God when He calls and letting God work His eternal purposes through our lives, for God's glory!

THOUGHT FOR THE DAY

God's purpose is for you to live with eternity in mind and not merely for "time."

Think about this past week, and consider how you invested your time. Make a list of the major activities you participated in, then place check marks beside the things you did that have eternal value.

❑ _____

❑ _____

❑ _____

❑ _____

Time invested in people can have eternal significance. How would you know if He is inviting you to encourage or disciple someone in your life? Spend time in prayer, asking God to open your eyes to people He has strategically placed in your life. Write down their names and ask God how you can minister to them this next week.

REVIEW YOUR MEMORY VERSE FOR THE WEEK.

And whatever you do, do it _____, as to the Lord and not to _____, knowing that from the Lord you will receive the _____ of the inheritance; for you serve the _____. COLOSSIANS 3:23–24

DAY 3
THE CALL OF GOD REQUIRES CHARACTER

God is seeking to develop the character of His Son Jesus in each of us. This is His eternal purpose. He would do through our lives what He was able to do through His Son.

God's goal for each believer is "to be conformed to the image of His Son" (Romans 8:29). "Image" can be understood as "characteristics." God is seeking to develop the character of His Son Jesus in each of us. As God shapes our character, we become better instruments to be used in His kingdom work. One of the characteristics of Jesus was His faithful obedience to do all that the Father asked of Him. Note these Scriptures:

In the days of His flesh . . . He had offered

up prayers and supplications, with vehement cries and tears to Him who was able to save Him from death, and was heard because of His godly fear, though He was a Son, yet He learned obedience by the things which He suffered. And having been perfected, He became the author of eternal salvation to all who obey Him. HEBREWS 5:7–9

Most assuredly, I say to you, the Son can do nothing of Himself, but what He sees the Father do; for whatever He does, the Son also does in like manner. John 5:19

Jesus answered them and said, "My teaching is not Mine, but His who sent me. If anyone wants to do His will, he shall know concerning the doctrine, whether it is from God or whether I speak on My own authority. He who speaks from himself seeks his own glory; but He who seeks the glory of the One who sent Him is true, and no unrighteousness is in Him." JOHN 7:16–18 (NIV)

The result of Christ's obedience was that the Father brought eternal salvation to the human race through the Son. As God's people are obedient to make their lives available to God in the same way His Son was available to Him, God will work through them to accomplish His eternal purposes.

Based on these Scriptures, describe Jesus' obedience to the Father:

_____

_____

_____

_____

Jesus obeyed the Father in every area of His life. He only did what the Father told Him to do; He only spoke what the Father told Him to speak; He only taught what the Father told Him to teach. Remember that God desires to create or build this same attitude for obedience into your life.

This is what Jesus prayed for all those who would follow Him:

Sanctify them by Your truth. Your word is truth. As You sent Me into the world, I also have sent them into the world. And for their sakes I sanctify Myself, that they also may be sanctified by the truth. JOHN 17:17–19

He wanted His disciples to be "set apart for God," in the same way that He was set apart for God. This is God's eternal purpose for each of our lives! This is a very serious and eternal purpose of God, to be worked out in our lives, as it was in Jesus' life. God is seeking to develop the character of His Son in us. It is important at this time in our study to examine this key passage in Romans:

We know that all things work together for good to those who love God, to those who are called according to His purpose. For those whom He foreknew, He also predestined to be conformed to the image of His Son, that He might be the firstborn among many brethren. Moreover whom He predestined, these He also called; whom He called, these He also justified; and whom He justified, these He also glorified. RO-MANS 8:28–30

This truth carries with it so much of the why of our being called of God. Such character is developed through our relationship with Him as He works out, in the middle of our everyday life, His eternal plan of redemption. He calls us into a relationship with Himself, so that in the relationship we can come to know Him and experience His working in us and through us. In that relationship, and only there, does He develop character in us in preparation for an eternity with Him. At this time in our study this may sound "very heavy" to you. It is — but it is the heart of the Christian's life!

THOUGHT FOR THE DAY

God is seeking to develop the character of His Son Jesus in each of us in order to work through our lives as He did through His Son.

Read John 17:1–26. As you read this prayer, remember that you were included in Jesus' heart and mind when He prayed this for His followers (notice v. 20).

List the characteristics Jesus prays that God would develop into His disciples. For example, in verse 3 He prays that they would come to "know" God and Jesus Christ. (You'll find Jesus' focus on His disciples in vv. 6–19.)

_____

_____

_____

_____

Not only did Jesus intercede for His disciples, but, Jesus lives to intercede for us — He is praying for you! (Hebrews 7:25; Romans 8:27, 34) You might have noticed in John 17 that He prayed some amazing things for His disciples including His desire that we become one with God in the same perfect union He has with the Father (v. 21).

As you look at the list you made from John 17, pray and ask God to show you areas in your life where He is developing these characteristics. List at least one example here.

_____

_____

_____

_____

Remember, you can't build these "characteristics" into your life by yourself — but we can partner with God as He develops our character.

I cannot do it alone;
The waves run fast and high,
And the fogs close all around,
The light goes out in the sky;
But I know that we two
Shall win in the end,
Jesus and I.

Coward and wayward and weak,
I change with the changing sky;
Today so eager and bright,
Tomorrow too weak to try;
But He never gives in,
So we two shall win,
Jesus and I.

I could not guide it myself,
My boat on life's wild sea;
There's One who sits by my side,
Who pulls and steers with me.
And I know that we two
Shall safe enter port,
Jesus and I.

Streams in the Desert, vol. 1, Mrs. Charles E.
Cowman, page. 386.

DAY 4
CONFORMED TO THE IMAGE OF CHRIST

The entire process of developing Christ-like character in every believer begins when God draws us to Himself in a relationship of love. He first redeems us from our sin, forgiving us and cleansing us and setting us apart for Himself. He places His Son in us (Colossians 1:27–29), and His Son begins to live out His life through us (Galatians 2:20), until each believer is "perfect [i.e., complete] in Christ" (Colossians 1:28). Paul told the Galatians, "until Christ is formed in you" (Galatians 4:19), he would labor with God tirelessly on their behalf.

⸺⸺⸺

The process of developing Christlike character in every believer begins when God calls us to Himself in a relationship of love.

⸺⸺⸺

Read Colossians 1:27–29; Galatians 2:20; and Romans 8:2. Then fill in the blanks.

To them God _____ to make known what are the riches of the glory of this mystery among the Gentiles; which is _____

I live by faith in the Son of God, who _____ me and _____Himself for me. Galatians 2:20

For the law of the Spirit of life in Christ Jesus _____ from the law of sin and death. ROMANS 8:2

The relationship of love that God initiates in believers continues throughout the rest of their lives. God develops us, equips us, and takes us on mission with Himself into our world. God is not willing that any should perish, in any generation or in any part of the world.

———

God is not willing that any should perish, in any generation or in any part of the world.

———

Throughout the Bible there are many persons God called to Himself. We could study any one of these persons and see this eternal purpose of God unfolding. The disciples that Jesus called to Himself provide a clear example. As Jesus called His disciples, He said, "Follow Me!" And they immediately left all and followed Him.

First, Jesus knew that each had been given to Him by the Father. At the close of His life, as He prayed in the Garden of Gethsemane, He affirmed it this way:

I have manifested Your name to the men whom You have given Me out of the world. They were Yours, You gave them to Me, and they have kept Your word. Now they have known that all things which You have given Me are from You. For I have given them the words which You have given Me; and they have received them, and have known surely that I came forth from You; and they have believed that You sent Me. JOHN 17:6–8

As You sent Me into the world, I also have sent them into the world. JOHN 17:18

So Jesus said to them again, "Peace to you! As the Father has sent Me, I also send you." JOHN 20:21

Second, Jesus knew absolutely that it was His assignment from the Father to prepare these men for the Father's eternal purpose. That purpose was to take the good news of His great salvation to the ends of the earth. This purpose would unfold after His assignment was completed to reconcile the world to God through the Cross, the Resurrection, and the Ascension. For the entire three and one-half years of Jesus' ministry this is what He did. He took the disciples with Him as He taught, preached, and healed. He revealed to them the Father, and the Father's purposes — and the disciples believed. When Jesus returned to the Father, He sent the disciples into the world, in the same way the Father had sent Him into the world (John 17:18; 20:21). The "keys of the kingdom of heaven" were in their hands (Matthew 16:19). They would be working with the Father and the Son, in the power of the Holy Spirit, to fulfill the Father's purpose to redeem a lost world to Himself.

In light of where He has placed you (family, church, workplace, neighborhood, etc.), do you believe God has an assignment for you?
❑ Yes
❑ No

❑ Maybe, but I'm not sure yet

This was the Father's way, and is still the Father's way, in each of our lives who believe in His Son, Jesus Christ. The Father draws us to His Son and gives us to Him. Jesus is still entrusted with receiving us from the Father and giving us eternal life (John 17:2–3). He continues teaching and guiding each believer, molding them as the Father has instructed Him until each knows the Father and responds to Him. Just as the early disciples experienced a relationship with Him, the more one responds, the more God uses that individual to go with Him on a redemptive mission to the ends of the earth. As the disciples obeyed the Lord in this relationship of love, God turned their world upside down (Acts 17:6). All through history, God has continued to do this, and desires once again in our generation to do this same work of love.

THOUGHT FOR THE DAY

Remember that God reveals His purposes to work through those He calls, and He is doing this in your life also. You have been given to His Son, and His Son knows what the Father has in mind for your life — in your generation. Today we saw how Jesus taught the disciples while He was on earth and how He prepared them to fulfill the Father's purpose in their generation.

Look back on your life experiences. Record a least one example of how God shaped your life in order send you out into the world to accomplish His purposes.

_____

_____

_____

_____

When God is shaping a person's life, at times, it can be difficult to recognize. In what circumstances do you currently find yourself? Could God be preparing you for something He will use your life to accomplish in the future? Take time to prayerfully consider how God is currently shaping your life to be more like His Son. Write your thoughts here.

_____

_____

_____

_____

*And whatever you do, do it _____,
as to the _____ and not to _____,
knowing that from the _____ you will receive the _____ of the inheritance; for
you serve the _____ _____.*
COLOSSIANS 3:23–24

DAY 5
CALLED, BECAUSE HE LOVES US!

This week we have studied several Scriptures related to the call of God on a person's life. We sought to understand God's call and apply it personally in relation to:

- Our role as a watchperson
- How we spend our time in light of eternity
- The character God builds into those He calls
- How He wants to conform us into the image of Jesus

We have laid the foundation that we will build upon in the coming weeks of our study together. Today we will focus on the fundamental truth that God calls us because He loves us. In the mind and heart of God so much is at stake when He calls a person! God's call to us is not merely so we can go to heaven when we die, but so that we can begin knowing Him, walking with Him, and serving Him from the time of salvation and throughout eternity. He desires a relationship with those He calls — a love relationship! Jesus is the pattern of love for us. He first loved us, drew us to Himself, adopted us into His family through salvation, and sent the Holy Spirit to reside in us so that we could experience and share His love with others. Jesus describes His love for us plainly in John 15:9–17.

Jesus said to him, " 'You shall love the Lord your God with all your heart, with all your soul, and with all your mind.' This is the first and great commandment. And the second is like it: 'You shall love your neighbor as yourself.' On these two commandments hang all the Law and the Prophets." MATTHEW 22:37–40

But concerning brotherly love you have no need that I should write to you, for you yourselves are taught by God to love one another; and indeed you do so toward all the brethren who are in all Macedonia. But we urge you, brethren, that you increase more and more; that you also aspire to lead a quiet life, to mind your own business, and to work with your own hands, as we commanded you, that you may walk properly toward those who are outside, and that you may lack nothing. 1 THESSALONIANS 4:9–12

Read John 15:9–17 in your Bible, then answer the following questions.

Jesus said that He loved us in the same way the Father loved Him. He tells the disciples to *abide* in His love. How can we *abide* in His love? (v. 10)

_____

_____

_____

_____

What is the result of keeping His commandments and abiding in His love? (v. 11)

_____

_____

_____

_____

When we obey Him, we will abide in His love and we will experience His joy

to the fullest measure. Jesus describes a new relationship He will have with His disciples. How does Jesus describe this new love relationship? (v. 15)

_____

_____

_____

_____

Jesus says that those who keep His commandments will no longer be called His servant or slave, but they will be called His friends. He goes on to describe this intimate friendship by telling the disciples that He will reveal all things that He hears from His Father to the one who abides in His love.

Let us illustrate this truth. A few years ago we had a family reunion in England. While we were there, we were able to tour Buckingham Palace and Windsor Castle. As we walked through the Queen's residences, we spoke with those who worked there. They told us so many things about the Queen that we didn't know. As we saw the beautiful rooms and read about all of the history that had taken place in each room, we were filled with excitement. We learned a lot about the Queen from those who worked for her. They knew her because they were with her when she resided at the palace; they served her. But they didn't know her like her children knew her. Her children knew her intimately and in ways that her workers would never know her. As children of God, we have the wonderful privilege of knowing the King of kings intimately. Not only do we serve Him, we are His children and have the privilege of sitting at His table and listening to Him each moment. We have access to His understanding and His wisdom.

THOUGHT FOR THE DAY

He chose us because He loved us! In the mind and heart of God so much was at stake when He called you. Think back over the last few weeks or months. Would you (or someone close to you) be able to describe your life as a life that *abides in God's love?*

_____

_____

_____

REVIEWING WEEK TWO

Look back over this week's lesson. Pray and ask God to reveal one (or more) statements or Scriptures that He wants you to understand, learn, or practice. **Write it on the** lines below.

_____

_____

_____

_____

Reword the statement or Scripture into a prayer of response to God.

_____

_____

_____

_____

What does God want you to do in response to this week's study? Are there adjustments you need to make to your schedule? Is there someone God has put in your path that you need to pray for, encourage, or witness to? (Take a moment to record this on the "Final Thoughts Summary" found on p. 284–285.)

_____

_____

_____

_____

Review this week's memory verse. Turn it into a prayer of response to God. For example:

"As I go to work today, help me to work with integrity, knowing that ultimately I serve and answer to You, Lord for my thoughts, actions, attitudes. Help me to represent You today as I work in the world. Amen."

_____

_____

_____

_____

"All This I Did for Thee, What Hast Thou Done for Me?"

Zinzendorf was born in 1700 in Dresden, Germany, into one of the noblest families of Europe. As a young adult, Nicholas visited an art museum in Düsseldorf, Germany, where he saw the painting by Domenico Feti titled Ecce Homo (Behold the Man). *The painting depicted the risen Christ with the legend, "All this I did for thee, what hast thou done for Me?" The face of Christ in the painting never left Nicholas Zinzendorf's heart, and Christ's love became the compelling force of his life. Zinzendorf's love for his Savior was expressed in his love for other believers, especially through a small group of approximately 300 Moravians whom he allowed to establish a church on his estate at Herrnhut in 1722. He helped the Moravians develop a deep passion for their Savior and helped them to live out Christ's command to love one another. Zinzendorf's love for Christ was also expressed through his life of prayer. He spent countless hours in communion with* his Savior and sought to lead others to commit to a life of prayer. His example led the Moravian believers to begin a powerful prayer movement they called "hourly intercession." They prayed in shifts, 24 hours a day, 7 days a week, for the work of Christ around the world. This "hourly intercession" went on uninterrupted for over 100 years!

Zinzendorf's passion for Jesus was also manifested in his desire to reach those who did not know his Savior. By 1752, the Moravian Church at Herrnhut had sent out more missionaries than the whole Protestant church had done in 200 years. Before long they had three members on the missions field for everyone at their church in Herrnhut. All this was accomplished by men and women with little formal and theological education, but with a burning passion for their Savior, Jesus Christ. Zinzendorf's life was a labor of love for his Savior, who had done so much for him and a lost and dying world.

UNIT THREE
WHAT IS A CALL?

MEMORY VERSE FOR THE WEEK

And this is eternal life, that they may know You, the only true God, and Jesus Christ whom You have sent. JOHN 17:3

ESSENTIAL TRUTH FOR THE WEEK

One must believe that God really does speak to us in this matter of His call. From Genesis through Revelation, no truth stands out any clearer than the truth that God *"speaks" to His people.* They always know that it is God, they know what He is saying, and they know how they are to respond. In other words, this is not just an academic exercise or merely a "theological truth." It is a real relationship with God, and He really does call each of us to Himself for His eternal purposes. This truth is foundational to our study of being called and accountable!

GOD GAVE HER A NEW ASSIGNMENT

Judith, a paralegal, was pregnant with her second child and driving to the law firm where she worked when she was suddenly struck with blindness. Within the next 24 hours, she experienced many physical problems that affected her hearing and her ability to walk. In one day, she lost her ability to work, her independence, her ability to see, and her ability to hear. This experience served as a wake-up call to Judith, showing her that God had a new direction for her life. God used these circumstances to bring her into a new realm in her relationship with Him. As Judith began to adjust to being legally blind and to her significant loss of hearing, she realized for the first time what it was like to be disabled. God gave her a desire to minister to people with disabilities and made her aware of the day-to-day difficulties they encounter in society. She became an encourager to the discouraged as she began to get involved in her city government as an advocate for the disabled.

Judith is very articulate and kind, and God gave her the words to speak to the city officials regarding some of the basic needs of the disabled. As a result of her obedience, the city of Phoenix made radical changes throughout the city to accommodate the disabled. Looking back, she says that "God's assignment was for her to put a face with a problem and to stand before the leaders to hold them accountable." She dealt with them as a Christian; she honored her Lord and He honored her. She built relationships with government leaders, became a friend to many on the city council, and has been appointed to leadership roles on several national boards relating to the disabled. She always knew that God had a plan for her life and her disabilities, but she had never really internalized what that meant. As she sought to study God's Word, and to take part in Bible studies with other believers, she realized that there were very few Christian resources for the legally blind. Thus, God has given her a new assignment: to work with Christian publishers to make discipleship material available for the disabled.

Judith is currently working with some people from the Christian Booksellers Association in hopes to make Christian publishers aware of the needs of the disabled regarding disciple-

ship material. Recently, Judith, with the help of two friends, translated Experiencing God: Knowing and Doing the Will of God *into Braille format. At the time of this printing, both* Experiencing God *and* Called and Accountable Devotional *are in Braille format and available through Assemblies of God Center for the Blind, 1445 N. Boonville Ave., Springfield, MO 65802; (417) 831-1964; blind@ag.org. God has used Judith's life to minister to and encourage thousands of people with disabilities — an ordinary person called by God!*

DAY 1
A CALL TO RELATIONSHIP

From the very beginning, in the Garden of Eden, we see God bringing Adam into being and "calling" him to Himself. It was preeminently a call to a love relationship with God. God created him in His love. He instructed Adam (and later, Eve) to partner with Him by naming the animals and by having dominion over all God had created (Genesis 1:28). God continued to give Adam and Eve instructions about the stewardship and accountability of their assignments. The character of God's perfect creation is found in the repetitive words, "God spoke! And it was so! And it was good!" This was supremely true about God's relationship of love with Adam and Eve. This is always true with God when He brings any person into His world! But sin entered into the lives of Adam and Eve, and the loving relationship with God was broken. One weeps just in reading again the pitiful picture of Adam and

Eve hiding themselves from the presence of God (Genesis 3:8). And then the heart cry of God, "Adam, where are you?" (Genesis 3:9–10). Adam and Eve were now afraid of God. What a change in relationship!

Then the Lord God called to Adam and said to him, "Where are you?" GENESIS 3:9

The rest of the Bible is the story of God pursuing this relationship of love with His children. In every generation God called His people to return to a love relationship with Him. The Bible is the story of God's redemptive love providing everyone who will believe Him a way back to His love. God provided salvation through His Son so that His eternal purpose of love could be restored. Too often people think of this salvation as simply providing a way to go to heaven at death. This is certainly a vital part of God's great salvation. However, as we have noted, God did not create us for time, but for eternity! It is important at this point in our study to keep in mind Jesus' definition of eternal life:

And this is eternal life, that they may know You, the only true God, and Jesus Christ whom You have sent. JOHN 17:3

The Bible is the story of God's redemptive love providing everyone who will believe Him a way back to His love.

What is the key phrase in Jesus' definition of eternal life?

_____ _____ _____ _____ _____

The key phrase is "that they may know You."

Write a definition of what you think "to know" means.

_____

_____

_____

_____

The Amplified Bible will help us to understand this definition more intimately. For example, in John 17:3 and Philippians 3:10, the Amplified Bible describes eternal life and what it means "to know" God the Father and Son.

And this is eternal life: [it means] to know (to perceive, recognize, become acquainted with and understand) You, the only true and real God, and [likewise] to know Him, Jesus [as the] Christ, the Anointed One, the Messiah, Whom You have sent. JOHN 17:3 (AMP)

[For my determined purpose is] that I may know Him — that I may progressively become more deeply and intimately acquainted with Him, perceiving and recognizing and understanding [the wonders of His Person] more strongly and more clearly. And that I may in that same way come to know the power out-flowing from His resurrection [which it exerts over believers]; and that I may so share His sufferings as to be continually transformed [in spirit into His likeness even] to His death. PHILIPPIANS 3:10 (AMP)

Based on these two Scriptures, are you sensing that eternal life through Christ is more than just going to heaven when you die?
❑ Yes
❑ No
❑ Maybe

God's call to His great salvation provided in His Son is an incredible expression of His eternal love for each of us. You catch the enormous nature of this relationship as the Apostle Paul bears witness to his new "life in Christ."

Using the following Scriptures, write down how Paul describes his "life in Christ."

1 Corinthians 15:9–10

_____

_____

_____

_____

Galatians 2: 19–20

_____

_____

_____

_____

Philippians 1:21

_____

_____

_____

_____

Philippians 4:19–26

_____

_____

_____

_____

_____

Paul's letters are full of such expressions of love to his Lord. He speaks out of his personal experience as he relates his gratitude to God and his desire to honor Him. As you read these Scriptures, did you catch Paul's desire to release his entire life in order to embrace all of God through this personal relationship? Jesus describes "life in Him" vividly in John 15.

Read John 15:1–11 and answer the following questions.

Jesus said that He was the Vine and that we are the branches and that we can do _____ without Him.
❑ not very much
❑ nothing

❑ some things
❑ most things

Often we know or have heard about these words of Jesus in John 15, but we don't make the connection to our daily life. Take time to be honest with God and describe your "life in Christ" or your relationship with Christ. As you do this, see if any of the Scriptures previously noted match with your own life.

Ask yourself these questions:
1. Do you enjoy spending time simply talking with your Lord?
2. Do you consider Him and His ways with all of the decisions you make?
3. Are you regularly resting in His peace?
4. Do you find yourself relying on His power and strength to carry you through each day?
5. Are His words increasingly becoming the standard for your words, actions, and thoughts?

_____

_____

_____

_____

_____

_____

_____

_____

When you read the testimonies of those in the Bible and in history who have described their relationship with God, they usually tell of the overwhelming relationship of love that took place when they were called of God.

THOUGHT FOR THE DAY

This "call" of God to every believer is to an intimate and life-giving relationship with God, which is totally life-transforming and ultimately world-changing with God.

Describe how God's love has transformed your life since you came into an intimate relationship with Christ.

_____

_____

_____

_____

_____

_____

REVIEW THIS WEEK'S MEMORY VERSE.

And this is _____ life, that they may _____ You, the only true God, and _____ _____ whom You have sent. JOHN 17:3

DAY 2
THE CALL IS REDEMPTIVE

There is another aspect of this relationship and calling, one that is so often overlooked or neglected: this relationship is always redemptive! This means that the call to salvation is at the same time a call to be on mission with God to reach the lost in the world. The moment any person is brought into a relationship with God, they experience the heart of God, the mind of God, and the eternal purposes of God. All that is on the heart of the Son of God, who now dwells within us through the Holy Spirit, increasingly becomes a part of our heart as well. (If you are unfamiliar with the role that the Holy Spirit has in guiding us to know what is on Jesus' heart, see John 16:13–15.) It is impossible to live intimately with God and not be "transformed into the same image from glory to glory, just as by the Spirit of the Lord" (2 Corinthians 3:18).

The call to salvation is at the same time a call to be on mission with God to reach the lost in the world.

As God transforms us, He lays His heart over ours and we begin to share His burdens — that He is "not willing that any should perish but that all should come to repentance" (2 Peter 3:9). God, who sent His only Son into the world that we, through Him, might be saved (John 3:16), will also send us into the world that others, through us, might be saved (by our witness to His great salvation).

This truth, again, is seen throughout the entire Bible, and all those mightily used throughout history bear witness to its reality. From the moment of salvation there should come over the new believer, a deep sense of being on mission with the Lord in their world. Many people indicate that at salvation they sensed a call to missions, evangelism, and witnessing. This is not surprising in light of God's heart for people.

From the moment of salvation there comes over the new believer a deep sense of being on mission with the Lord in their world.

—————

In Philippians 2:3–11, Paul urged the believers in the church at Philippi to "let this mind be in you which was also in Christ Jesus" (v. 5) and then he listed what this would mean specifically. He expected Christ to be formed in them, so he urged them to let Him do so. Then he added,

> *Work out your own salvation with fear and trembling; for it is God who works in you both to will and to do for His good pleasure.* PHILIPPIANS 2:12–13

Read Hebrews 13:20–21. Write down what the author of Hebrews prayed God would do in the their lives:

_____

_____

_____

_____

Yes, He wants to "make you complete in every good work, working in you what is well pleasing in His sight." And He does it to bring glory to the Father.

This means that each believer must let the full implications of their salvation work into every area of their life. Each Christian must respond to Him as Lord over all of their life, remembering that "for it is God who works in you both to will and to do for His good pleasure" (Philippians 2:13). What an exciting truth for every believer!

Let me illustrate this process from the life of a friend named John who was working as a personal bodyguard for a member of a high profile family in Texas. Earlier in John's life he had sensed a call to missions and ministry, but through the years he had wandered away from God and was not serving as God had intended. Through circumstances out of John's control, he was falsely accused of some things and demoted to sitting in a guard shack outside of one of the family's homes. During this time he had the option to become angry, but instead he looked to God for understanding. God assured John that the call to be on mission had not changed after all of the wasted years. John released his life to the Lord and renewed his commitment to the call. Within a short time a ministry contacted John to serve by working with boys and men. Over the years, John has traveled the country helping men and boys walk with God. To look over his life is to see that God had never released him from the call and was working in his life to cause him to will and want to follow God's claim on his life.

Throughout the Bible and throughout history, those mightily used of God have had this same pattern in their lives. Both of our Christian lives began with a deep sense that God had something in mind when He saved us (John 15:16).

You did not choose Me, but I chose you and appointed you that you should go and bear fruit, and that your fruit should remain, that whatever you ask the Father in My name He may give you. JOHN 15:16

Henry recalls, anything that God presented to me, I responded to Him as His servant. I began by leading youth. As I led the youth I watched for anything God would desire to do through my life. Then a church asked if I would be their music/education director. It never crossed my mind not to respond, for I knew that the call to salvation was at the same time the call to serve with God in my world.

Two years later, that same church asked if I

would be their pastor. After years of pastoring, some churches asked if I would be their director of missions. I agreed and served for six years. Then a national missions agency asked if I would guide our convention toward prayer and spiritual awakening. I did that with them, as well as worked with an international missions agency until April of 2000.

No matter what assignment God has given me over the past 50 years of ministry, I have always responded to Him as His servant. And He has always been faithful to equip me for whatever assignment He gives.

THOUGHT FOR THE DAY

It is an awesome truth that the God of the universe has called you to be on mission with Him in your world. When He calls you, He is inviting you to follow Him. Accepting this invitation will require you to make adjustments in your life.

As you look back over the past few months or years, you probably recognize many times when God invited you to be on mission with Him. What adjustments did your obedience to follow Him cause you to make? (You might think of this in terms of your family, workplace,

community, or church; or, in terms of acquiring additional training, a relocation, or a change in career your path.)

_____

_____

_____

_____

Pray and ask God to show you areas where He is inviting you to join Him this week. What adjustments will you need to make to join Him in His activity?

_____

_____

_____

_____

_____

_____

_____

If you cannot see where God is inviting you, then take time to ask God to help you "work out your salvation with Him" so that you will be ready for His next invitation.

DAY 3
A CALL TO MISSION

Every Christian is called to be on mission with God in our world. This is what it means to be called. God is seeking to bring a lost world back to Himself. He loves every person and He is not willing that any should perish. He has always been working in our world to seek and to save those who are lost. That is what He was doing when He called you! Those He saves, He involves as fellow workers with Himself in His eternal purpose to save a lost world.

But to every sincere Christian in every succeeding generation, Paul adds significantly, "Behold, now is the acceptable time; behold, now is the day of salvation" (2 Corinthians 6:2). In other words, the moment of their call was the moment God would be at work to redeem their world. It would be God's strategic moment of favor toward the people to whom the gospel would be preached. Paul knew this through experience, for he was living as a "worker with God." He was not only invited to "join God" but was given the enabling grace to be used to bring multitudes to salvation.

Read Matthew 1:18–2:23 in your Bible and answer the following questions. As you consider Joseph's response to God, take specific notice of verses 1:24, 2:14, 2:21, and 2:22.

What was about to take place when God came to Joseph?

_____

_____

_____

_____

How much time did Joseph have to respond to God's activity?

_____

_____

_____

_____

What could the outcome have been had

he not recognized the immediacy of the hour and not stepped out in faith quickly?

_____

_____

_____

_____

How important was it that Joseph obey God's instructions immediately? Check one:
- ❏ The timing of his obedience didn't really matter.
- ❏ His obedience was important, but the timing wasn't.
- ❏ His immediate obedience meant life or death to his family.

In the same way, when God speaks to us, the timing is critical and the lives of those closest to us may depend on our quick faith and obedience. When God gives you an assignment you can trust that His timing is perfect!

Has God instructed you to do something recently? How did you respond? Did you recognize the importance of the timing of God's instructions as they fit into His eternal plans? Take some time now to pray and ask God if there are any areas that He has instructed you and you have not responded. **If God brings to mind some areas where you have not responded yet, write them down and ask the Lord to help you adjust your life immediately to His will.**

_____

_____

_____

_____

_____

_____

_____

Immediate obedience will affect every area of your life — your family, your church, your community, and your workplace.

We work with people from all walks of life . . . single moms, doctors, truck drivers, teachers, repairmen, mechanics, pharmacists, small business owners, and CEOs. Each of these strategic men and women have been placed in the workplace by God for such a time as this! God is touching their minds and hearts deeply. They have an inner sense that God not only is at work in them and around them, but that God clearly wants greater access to work His kingdom purposes through them. They are "seeking the Lord with all their hearts" as God said He would cause them to do. And they are readying their lives, their marriages, their homes, and their business lives to be available to God in a maximum way. Month after month we hear how God is using them to accomplish His purposes in our day throughout the world.

I am hearing this same pattern of God's activity in teenagers in their schools, in college students on their campuses, and in so many women who believe that God is about to work toward a great revival in the nation through women wholly available to God. I believe this may be a vital part of God's strategy for redeeming our world in our day.

You may feel like your life cannot make a significant difference. However, God has strategically placed you around people whose life will be impacted by your life. This may happen through a word spoken at the right time that causes a person to make a life altering decision.

There is a sudden and extensive move of God, causing every believer to sense that their life is indeed "on mission with God" at this time.

God is truly on mission with His people in our day. There is no sense that only a few are called! All are called, and each Christian is urged to "walk worthy of the calling" (Ephesians 4:1–3).

How did the people described in the following verses "walk worthy of the calling"?

1 Thessalonians 1:6–8

_____

_____

_____

_____

_____

2 Timothy 4:6–8

_____

_____

_____

_____

_____

_____

_____

_____

_____

_____

The people of Thessalonica received the word and became an example to all believers in such a powerful way that Paul describes it as "the word of the Lord sounded forth" from them. Philemon was known as one who "refreshed the hearts of the saints." And Paul describes himself at the end of his life as having "fought the good fight." In addition, he realized that he was finishing the race (the calling or life-assignment) God had given him. Notice that all three passages describe how these men encouraged fellow believers.

Spend some time asking God if your life can be described as "walking worthy of the calling with which you were called."

Write down the areas where you can see that your life is pleasing to God and spend time thanking God for strengthening you to honor Him. Also, write down the areas where you see that you

have not been walking worthy of His call. Take time to repent of any sins He reveals to you and then ask God to help you turn these areas completely over to Him.

_____

_____

_____

_____

_____

_____

_____

DAY 4
GOD INITIATES THE CALL

In this entire process, God takes the initiative to come to His people and to let them know what He is doing or about to do. He came to Noah at the moment He was about to judge the world by a flood. Unless God had come to him, Noah could not have known what was about to happen. But Noah did know because God wanted to accomplish His purpose through Noah. So God gave Noah an assignment, and Noah responded as a co-worker with God.

When God was about to free His people from slavery in Egypt, He took the initiative to come to Moses and let Moses know what He was about to do. This revelation was God's invitation for Moses to work with Him to accomplish His purposes for His people. God came this way to each of the prophets.

Read the following verses and notice how God initiated the relationship and

the call of the following people.
Luke 5:1–11 — Simon Peter, James, and John
Matthew 9:9 — Matthew
Jeremiah 1:4–10 — Jeremiah
Jonah 1:1–2 — Jonah

Can you see from these examples that God takes the initiative? God encountered each person right in the middle of their daily routine, brought them to Himself, and then used them to accomplish His work.

To the disciples Jesus said, "You did not choose Me, but I chose you and appointed you that you should go and bear fruit, and that your fruit should remain, that whatever you ask the Father in My name He may give you" (John 15:16). To the apostle Paul and to God's people throughout history, this pattern is found every time He is about to do a great work in our world and it is still true today. It is true right now for your life as well!

God chooses us so that our lives will bear fruit. Describe your definition of "bearing fruit" in the Christian's life.

_____

_____

_____

_____

At times it may be hard to understand what "fruit" looks like in our lives. Certainly a good place to start is Galatians 5:22–23: "But the fruit of the spirit is love, joy, peace, longsuffering, kindness, goodness, faithfulness, gentleness, self-control." As God calls you and begins to work in your life so that He can use your life, you should see these characteristics growing in your life.

Take some time to evaluate your life to see if these characteristics are "growing" in your life. Write down which ones are evident in your life and which ones are not evident.

_____

_____

_____

_____

There are other kinds of "fruit" that our lives should be producing along with those listed in Galatians. Read the following Scriptures and write down what they say about "fruit" in the Christians life.

Colossians 1:10-12

_____

_____

_____

_____

_____

Philippians 1:11

_____

_____

_____

_____

James 3:17–18

_____

_____

_____

_____

Romans 7:4–6

_____

_____

_____

_____

_____

_____

_____

_____

_____

When God chose us He also designed our lives to bear fruit. **This fruit includes our character as well as our service to God in His work.** With the strong emphasis that Jesus placed on Christians bearing fruit (Luke 13:6–9; Matthew 3:10), it is important to look and see what your life is yielding.

In addition, this call of God will always involve some kind of major adjustment in your life to be the person God can use to accomplish His purposes. Moses had to leave herding sheep. David could not be a shepherd and be king at the same time. The disciples of Jesus could no longer continue fishing and go with Jesus at the same time. In our day, when lawyers, doctors, school-teachers, truck drivers, salespeople, nurses, or bankers become Christians, they respond to Christ as Lord over all of their lives, so He can accomplish His plans through His people.

142

What major adjustments is God asking you to make in your life so that He can bear maximum fruit through you?

_____

_____

_____

_____

God may leave Christians in their present vocation or professional position. However, it will not be "business as usual," or business as the world around them would have it. They will thoroughly realize that they have been "bought with a price," and therefore they are, at all times and in all places, to make sure that they seek to serve God (living out the call in every setting). That makes their workplace a place where God can accomplish His eternal purposes through them. The classroom becomes a "workplace for God" for one called to be a teacher or student. The workshop is God's place of evangelism for a car mechanic. The doctor's office or surgery suite becomes God's workplace for a medical doctor or nurse. The lawyer's office or courtroom for the lawyer or judge, and the halls of government for the congressman or mayor or political official, all become God's workplace. But the choice, the arena of activity God chooses for each believer, is entirely up to God.

———⚊⚊———

The arena of activity God chooses for each believer is entirely up to God.

———⚊⚊———

One of the greatest developments today is the tremendous number of missions volunteers who are leaving all and following Jesus — across North America and around the world. Teachers are going into China so that our Lord can reach Chinese people through them. Businesspeople are making their lives available through their work connections around the world so Christ can bring lost persons to Himself who would not hear any other way. Tens of thousands of volunteers are going around the world each year with a deep sense of being on mission with their Lord. What a difference this is making in our generation!

My wife, Dana, worked for a railroad for several years while I was in seminary. Her responsibilities changed as the railroad she worked for merged with another railroad. She was moved into a new position where she managed the severance packages for both companies. God put her in that position and used her to touch many people who were losing their jobs. One person affected by the lay-offs was a Christian woman whom God used in a very special way to touch the people of India. As she had the opportunity to get to know my wife, she shared with her a burden God had laid on her heart to send *Experiencing God* to her denominational missionaries in India. Here she was with a burden to get *Experiencing God* to the missionaries without any idea how to do it. Now, in the process of working through her severance package, she was introduced to the author's daughter-in-law. God had more than "severance packages" in mind when He placed Dana in that position.

She and Dana worked together and God led them to a printer who would print the book in the language of preference for each of their missionaries. Over 5,000 copies of *Experiencing God* were provided to these missionaries. God used a woman who lost her job to bring the message of knowing and doing God's will to thousands of people in India. When people are available to God, God can and will complete His work through them. This is a prime example of allowing God to work all things together for good in those who are called and account-able!

THOUGHT FOR THE DAY

When believers are available to God, God can and will complete His work through them (John 12:24–26).

Spend some time praying and ask God to show you how He is working through your life where He has placed you? List your thoughts in the space below.

_____

_____

_____

_____

_____

As you prayed, did God show you any adjustments He is asking you to make today? List your thoughts here.

_____

_____

_____

_____

REVIEW THIS WEEK'S MEMORY VERSE.

And this is _____ _____,
that they may _____ You, the
_____ _____ _____,
and _____ whom You have sent. JOHN
17:3

DAY 5
A CALL TO OBEDIENCE:
"YES, LORD!"

If believers were to think carefully about their present relationship with God, they would realize that their greatest challenge is not that they do not know the will of God, but rather that they do know His will but have not been willing to obey Him! Neither God nor history waits on a believers' responses to God's call and claim on their lives.

For many, the greatest challenge is not that they do not know the will of God, but rather that they do know His will but have not been willing to obey to Him!

God's call requires only one response from every believer — obedience! Once you, as a

148

child of God, recognize the activity of God in your life, you must immediately, without resistance or discussion, respond obediently to all God is directing. Only then will you experience God's working mightily through your life. There are times when we can tend to take our obedience to God lightly. However, God views our obedience as an essential key to our relationship with Him.

Look at the following Scriptures and write down how God views our obedience or disobedience to Him.

John 14:15–24

_____

_____

_____

1 Peter 1:13–16

_____

_____

_____

Romans 6:16–18

_____

1 Samuel 15:22

Our obedience to Christ is foundational. If we love Him, we will obey Him immediately! Our obedience is better than any offering we could possibly make. This was true in the life of Hudson Taylor. He was training as a medical doctor. When God made it unmistakably clear that He wanted to reach the peoples of inland China with the gospel through Taylor's life, Hudson Taylor was obedient. God did reach hundreds of thousands, even millions, of precious Chinese people through his life and those God would bring alongside him to preach, teach, and heal in China.

Further, a call from God always involves the person in the corporate life of the people of God. Even God's call to Abram involved all the people of God who would follow Abram. God's call to Moses directly involved God's purposes in the life of Israel, His people.

God's call — to Joshua, the judges, Samuel, David, the prophets, the disciples, and Paul — brought them into the midst of what God had purposed to do through their lives.

In what ways does the manner you follow God impact other Christians around you? Think about this in light of co-workers, neighbors, relatives, and friends.

_____

_____

_____

_____

_____

_____

In the New Testament, the redemptive work of God was to be lived out through the life of His people functioning together in local churches. Through these churches, God would take His great salvation to the ends of the earth. Every believer should anticipate that God will involve them dynamically in their local church. God will then, as He did in the New Testament, involve each church in the life of sister churches that He has established in His kingdom. This will involve linking with churches and people from other denominations, as well.

THOUGHT FOR THE DAY

Obedience is always the key to experiencing a life on mission with God in our world!

Describe a recent time when you stepped out in obedience to God and experienced Him working through you to help others.

_____

_____

_____

_____

Did your obedience effect/impact the life of your church or small group?

_____

_____

_____

_____

Is there any area of your life in which God is clearly inviting you to follow Him, but you have not yet responded? If

so, respond to Him now.

_____

_____

_____

_____

REVIEWING WEEK THREE

Look back over this week's lesson. Pray and ask God to reveal one (or more) statements or Scriptures that He wants you to understand, learn, or practice. **Write it on the lines below.**

_____

_____

_____

_____

Reword the statement or Scripture into a prayer of response to God.

_____

_____

_____

_____

What does God want you to do in response to this week's study? (Take a

moment to record this on the "Final Thoughts Summary" found on p. 284–285.)

_____

_____

_____

_____

Review this week's memory verse. Turn it into a prayer of response to God.

_____

_____

_____

_____

RON MARTIN

USED BY GOD AT WORK — EVERY DAY!

Many years ago I was asked to lead a weekly spiritual leadership class at our church. On the first day, I wondered who would show up for the class and what would come from this study. Several people showed up the first night from a wide variety of backgrounds. About 20 minutes into our first meeting a middle aged man named Ron walked in dressed in a Fed Ex uniform. He apologized for being late and explained that he was a truck driver for Fed Ex and that he may be late at times due to the amount of packages on his route. After the first night, I sat with my wife, Dana and told her about the group. There were several leaders from the church in attendance and a couple prominent businessmen. I wondered what God was going to do through this class to impact our church and community. Little did I know that the one individual that God would shape and use to impact countless lives (including my own) was Ron.

During our time in the class and months following there was a significant transformation in Ron's life. He was taking God's word seriously and committing to practice all he was learning. Ron, looking back over his life, described himself as a "a difficult guy that was pretty angry." He shared some of the difficulties he had with family and various people, but now he was experiencing a radical change in his heart. His love for God and others was rapidly growing in a way that was impacting his Bible study, prayer life, family life, and work. God began a wonderful transformation in Ron, conforming him to the image of Christ. However, this transformation was not simply for Ron, but for all of the people God wanted to impact through his life.

God did not remove Ron from his job, but began to use him and continues to use him at his workplace. He began to be burdened for customers when he realized he was delivering medicine for people with cancer or other diseases. As a result, he began to offer to pray with people along his route. Ron recounts that he would have regular customers waiting for him to come by on his route so they could share what God had done in their lives after he had prayed for them. While he had to make sure he was staying on time with his deliveries, he regularly found himself encountering people in great need. He simply offered to pray with them and would share an encouraging word concerning God's love. Not only has God used Ron to impact his customers, but his co-workers, from his bosses to fellow drivers, began to seek him out for prayer and encouragement. He finds people dropping by or waiting at his truck in the mornings to share their burdens, knowing that Ron will pray for them (and that Ron's prayers make a difference).

Over the years, Ron and I have continued to remain friends. I can say without question that each time we talk, a majority of our time is spent with Ron telling me about all of the activity of God (the way God is using him with customers and his co-workers). Ron continues to be amazed as to why these people seek him out for prayer and help. However, it is not very difficult to understand why. You see, when Ron allowed God to change his heart, it was to shape him to be used by God to help hurting people. The call was to a relationship, not an assignment. Ron simply had to allow God to shape his heart and then God opened his eyes to see what He was doing in the people that were already around him.

UNIT FOUR
HOW AM I CALLED?

———◦◦◦———

MEMORY VERSE FOR THE WEEK

If anyone serves Me, let him follow Me; and where I am, there My servant will be also. If anyone serves Me, him My Father will honor. JOHN 12:26

ESSENTIAL TRUTH FOR THE WEEK

Each child of God must learn to hear and recognize the voice of God.

But blessed are your eyes because they see, and your ears because they hear. For truly I tell you, many prophets and righteous people longed to see what you see but did not see it, and to hear what you hear but did not hear it. MATTHEW 13:16–17 (NIV)

HAROLD RAY WATSON
A New Way to Be Salt

In 1965 Harold Watson, his wife, Joyce, and their three small boys arrived in M'lang, Cotabato, a small town in the center of Mindanao, the Philippines. Harold and his family had been appointed by the International Mission Board to be "agriculture evangelists" on the second largest island in the Philippines.

Harold had never heard of agricultural evangelism while growing up on a farm in rural Mississippi. He liked farming and wondered if someday he might be able to have his own farm. While serving in the air force on the island of Okinawa during the Korean War, Harold believed that God was calling him to be a missionary. Harold began to think that there might be a new way to share the gospel of Jesus Christ in foreign lands through his love of farming.

Upon arriving in the Philippines, Harold observed that many of the Filipinos were impoverished and malnourished. Most of the steep

161

land was not suited for traditional farming, so the people had little to eat and no way to make even a meager income. Harold decided to set up a demonstration farm on 50 acres of land and develop a method of farming that would help the Filipinos be able to help themselves.

The 50 acres of land became known as the Mindanao Baptist Rural Life Center. Harold gradually developed a farming method called SALT (Sloping Agricultural Land Technology) which enables local farmers to produce food on badly eroded hillsides. Training programs at the center introduce people to the new farming method and to Jesus Christ. The students return to their villages with the ability to provide physical and spiritual food for their families. SALT has been adopted by a variety of countries and relief organizations to battle hunger, including Indonesia, Sri Lanka, Burma, and many other Asian countries. Some 18,000 people visit the center every year to learn SALT.

Jesus commanded His followers to be the "salt of the earth." God showed Harold Watson a new way to be salt in a lost world.

DAY 1
AWARENESS OF GOD'S CALL

For a Christian to seriously ask the question, "How am I called?" they must first approach this question with a personal commitment both to respond and to be accountable to God in the calling. When Christians sense that God is guiding them to a clear, simple answer to this question, they will also be deeply, even painfully aware that having the knowledge of His will brings with it a sense of accountability.

Having the knowledge of His will immediately brings with it a solemn sense of accountability.

At the moment when you sense God is calling you, you can never be the same again! You will have to make a conscience decision

163

to say, "Yes, Lord!" Be aware that you may tend to say no. But you cannot say, "No, Lord!" For if you say no, at that moment He is no longer Lord of your life. When Jesus is Lord, His servant is always striving to say, "Yes, Lord!"

We have already indicated that the initial call is a call to salvation, a call to become a child of God and servant of Jesus Christ. It is an eternal decision and an eternal relationship. But from the moment when you are born again, how are you called by God and placed on mission with Him?

Many forget that when a person first becomes a Christian, they are a "baby" Christian, and they must then grow and learn to use their newly given "spiritual senses." They need to learn to function with their newly provided spiritual family, the local church. This takes time and experience, just as it does in the physical birth and growth experience.

The context for this growth, as designed and provided by God, is the local church. God does not bring a person into His kingdom without adequate provision for protection, learning, feeding, and being loved. In the local church we learn about our new life in Christ and are given the opportunities to learn to walk, talk, share, and gain experiences.

New believers must first receive the "milk of the word" (1 Peter 2:2). As they grow, they are carefully taken from milk to meat.

Read Hebrews 5:12–14 and answer the following questions.

How would you describe your spiritual walk? Are you needing milk or meat?

_____

_____

_____

_____

Based on these verses, what are the distinguishing characteristics between a person on milk or meat?

_____

_____

_____

_____

Someone on "meat" would be a teacher of the Word, or someone who is continually moving beyond the beginning truths of the faith, who puts into practice and applies the truths of God consistently.

> *Not that I have already attained, or am already perfected; but I press on, that I may lay hold of that for which Christ Jesus has also laid hold of me. Brethren, I do not count myself to have apprehended; but one thing I do, forgetting those things which are behind and reaching forward to those things which are ahead, I press toward the goal for the prize of the upward call of God in Christ Jesus. Therefore let us, as many as are mature, have this mind; and if in anything you think otherwise, God will reveal even this to you.* PHILIPPIANS 3:12–15

Often we can think we are mature in the faith simply because we have been Christians for many years. However, the Bible describes maturity by how we learn and understand the Word of God, implement the truths of God into our lives, and allow God to use us to teach others to grow in the faith. **It is important to note that this passage in Hebrews was an address to** *all* the people and *not simply the leaders.* Each person was expected to grow and, in turn, teach others who were young in the faith. They should become teachers of the word, and by skillful use of the word move from milk to meat. The church must help each believer grow this way, becoming mature and able to be of greater use to God. Paul often spoke about becoming "mature" (Philippians 3:12–16; 1 Corinthians 14:20).

But all this takes time! It also takes obedience to Christ, who commanded believers not only to "make disciples" and "baptize them," but also to "teach them to observe all things that I have commanded you" (Matthew 28:19–20). This task is spiritually demanding but was faithfully practiced by early believers in Jerusalem, as seen in Acts 2:41–47. This is a simple and clear picture of a spiritual family, the local church, taking care of newborn believers. As you read the rest of the Book of Acts, you see how those believers soon were on mission with God all over their world. God really did accomplish His eternal purpose to redeem the lost through them.

I remember when Mark came to me with a burden to start a men's Bible study. He did not have much of a background in church and asked if I would be willing to lead the Bible study portion of the group if he coordinated the meetings and invited people to attend. One night after the Bible study, I received a phone call from Mark explaining that one of the people attending had called him asking for help. This person called Mark and wanted to know how to become a Christian. Mark told the man that he would call me and that I would contact the man immediately. When Mark called, he explained that I needed to call this person immediately because he was ready to become a Christian.

After talking with Mark, I explained that this was God's invitation for him to lead his friend to the Lord — not mine. Mark was not prepared for my response. I explained that God had put it upon his heart to start the group and that God had put it on this man's heart to call him and not me. So, I explained that I was going to hang up and go to bed. It was his responsibility to call the man back and share the gospel with him. Then I hung up the phone. You see, I did not want him to miss out on the privilege of leading someone to a personal faith in Christ.

The phone rang a little while later and the first words I heard were, "Norm, first you're a jerk!" And then, "But, thank you." Mark had called the man back and shared the good news with him, and the man had come to faith in Christ. I could have called the man and shared the good news with him. But, I knew Mark would miss out on the joy of leading his friend to the Lord. You see,

Mark did not recognize that God was inviting him to be a part of this man's salvation. I love to share the gospel and love to lead people to the Lord, but I was not about to let Mark miss out on this wonderful experience simply because he did not feel qualified to share the gospel.

Read Acts 2:41–47 and list the things the early church did to help their members mature in Christ.

_____

_____

_____

_____

Is the church you are a part of helping the members to grow into maturity? If it is, how are you helping in this discipleship process?

_____

_____

_____

_____

If your church is not helping its members to grow into maturity, how can

your life be used in the spiritual growth of the people?

_____

_____

_____

_____

A brief summary of the things that new believers must learn early in their Christian life would include:

- to receive spiritual food
- to develop their newly given "spiritual senses" (more about this in Day 2's study)
- to develop a great sensitivity toward sin
- to learn the strategies of Satan (as Jesus did)
- to learn to resist Satan and sin with their whole being
- to know (often the hard way) the consequences of sin, and the crucial place of the church in restoring them
- to know the nature of a life of holiness, so they will always be available to God
- to know their place in the body (local church) and how their lives are used by God to edify and grow others in the body

- to find out, as the disciples did, the nature of the kingdom of heaven, and how God functions in their world, especially through prayer
- to know how to effectively share their faith and present the gospel to others

Once a person begins to grow in Christ, they will be gradually taken on mission with God. As they are faithful in little things, God will give them more significant opportunities to be on mission with Him. In this process they will learn to "wait on the Lord" — to "be still." In this waiting they will come to learn to:

1. Yield their lives completely to God's working through them.
2. Appropriate all that God has provided by His grace and by His presence with them. This will include Christ living out His life in them, and the complete sufficiency of the presence and power of the Holy Spirit.

All this, and much more, is involved in an awareness of God's call.

THOUGHT FOR THE DAY
God's desire is that, once you have entered

into a relationship with Him, you would grow into maturity in the Christian life and, in turn, be used to help others grow in their faith.

Spend time praying and ask God if He is pleased with your growth as a Christian. Write down what He says here.

_____

_____

_____

_____

Have you released your life to God so that He can use you to help others grow in your church, neighborhood, or workplace? Ask God to show you how He wants to use you to help others grow, and write down any specific person that God places on your heart that you need to encourage.

_____

_____

_____

_____

DAY 2
SPIRITUAL SENSES DEVELOPED

A newborn child is fully equipped with senses to function in the physical world. By the constant use of them, a child grows to maturity. I had to assist each of my children as they used their eyes to see, their ears to hear, and their noses to smell. At each stage of their growth, they had new things to learn. I knew that if they grew normally, they could read and eventually attain a PhD, if God called them to that task. Each of my children have gone on to receive seminary training and are all serving the Lord. But the day-by-day growth when they were younger was essential to what they would become.

For everyone who partakes only of milk is unskilled in the word of righteousness, for he is a babe. But solid food belongs to those who are of full age, that is, those who by reason of use have their senses

exercised to discern both good and evil.
HEBREWS 5:13–14

⊸⊸⟋⟍⊷

Each child of God must learn to hear and recognize the voice of God, and obey Him.

⊸⊸⟋⟍⊷

Every believer must be helped to develop their spiritual senses, given to them by God. It is crucial to their development and their later usefulness to God. The local church is a major factor, as are the believers God places around them at spiritual birth.

Each child of God must learn to hear and recognize the voice of God, and obey Him. Jesus assured the disciples that this would be true when He said:

But he who enters by the door is the shepherd of the sheep. To him the doorkeeper opens, and the sheep hear his voice; and he calls his own sheep by name and leads them out. And when he brings out his own sheep, he goes before them; and the sheep follow him, for they know his voice. . . . My sheep hear My voice, and I know them, and they follow Me. JOHN 10:2–4, 27

Put this passage into your own words as it relates to you and your personal relationship with Christ.

_____

_____

_____

_____

Are you coming to sense the personal nature of your relationship with Christ when He called you? As you mature in this relationship, developing your spiritual senses, you will come to hear, recognize, and understand the voice of God as He seeks to use your life for His purposes.

Every sheep who is a part of His flock knows the Shepherd's voice and follows Him. Other sheep in the same fold can assist the lambs as they learn this skill.

Every sheep who is a part of His flock knows the Shepherd's voice and follows Him. Other

175

sheep in the same fold can assist the lambs as they learn this skill.

And the disciples came and said to Him, "Why do You speak to them in parables?" He answered and said to them, "Because it has been given to you to know the mysteries of the kingdom of heaven, but to them it has not been given. For whoever has, to him more will be given, and he will have abundance; but whoever does not have, even what he has will be taken away from him. Therefore I speak to them in parables, because seeing they do not see, and hearing they do not hear, nor do they understand." MATTHEW 13:10–13

To whom did Jesus give the ability to understand the ways and thinking of His kingdom?

_____

_____

_____

_____

It was the ones whom God had called, and once called, they chose to follow Christ — the disciples.

"And in them the prophecy of Isaiah is fulfilled, which says: 'Hearing you will hear and shall not understand, and seeing you will see and not perceive; for the hearts of this people have grown dull. Their ears are hard of hearing, and their eyes they have closed, lest they should see with their eyes and hear with their ears, lest they should understand with their hearts and turn, so that I should heal them.' But blessed are your eyes for they see, and your ears for they hear; for assuredly, I say to you that many prophets and righteous men desired to see what you see, and did not see it, and to hear what you hear, and did not hear it."
MATTHEW 13:14–16

Why were these people unable to see, hear, and receive healing from God?

_____

_____

_____

_____

What role does your "heart" play in hearing and following God's call on your life?

_____

"Therefore hear the parable of the sower: When anyone hears the word of the kingdom, and does not understand it, then the wicked one comes and snatches away what was sown in his heart. This is he who received seed by the wayside. But he who received the seed on stony places, this is he who hears the word and immediately receives it with joy; yet he has no root in himself, but endures only for a while. For when tribulation or persecution arises because of the word, immediately he stumbles. Now he who received seed among the thorns is he who hears the word, and the cares of this world and the deceitfulness of riches choke the word, and he becomes unfruitful. But he who received seed on the good ground is he who hears the word and understands it, who indeed bears fruit and produces: some a hundredfold, some sixty, some thirty." MATTHEW 13:16–23

Jesus clearly indicated to His disciples that since they had been "called by

God," they were different in several significant ways. In what ways were they different?

_____

_____

_____

_____

You're right, they could "know the mysteries of the kingdom of heaven, but to them [others around them] it has not been given" (Matthew 13:11). This was followed by an astounding announcement: "But blessed are your eyes for they see, and your ears for they hear" (Matthew 13:16). Every believer must develop the use of these special spiritual senses. It is by the use of them that one grows (Hebrews 5:13–14).

Look up the following verses and list ways our spiritual senses help us in our relationship with God.

John 10: 2–4, 27

_____

_____

_____

_____

John 5:17; 19–20

_____

_____

_____

_____

John 16:13–15

_____

_____

_____

_____

Our spiritual senses help us to hear His voice and follow Him; to see His activity and join Him; and to have hearts that understand and obey Him.

Just as a little child learns to function in our world a little at a time, if we are faithful in a little, He will give us more (Luke 16:10). Jesus said that when we hear and then obey, we are like a man building his house on a rock — nothing can shake it or destroy it (Luke 6:46–49).

But why do you call Me "Lord, Lord," and not do the things which I say? Whoever comes to Me, and hears My sayings and does them, I will show you whom he is like:

180

he is like a man building a house, who dug deep and laid the foundation on the rock. And when the flood arose, the stream beat vehemently against that house, and could not shake it, for it was founded on the rock. But he who heard and did nothing is like a man who built a house on the earth without a foundation, against which the stream beat vehemently; and immediately it fell. And the ruin of that house was great.
LUKE 6:46–49

There are some things that must be firmly in place in the Christian's life to experience the fullness of God's calling in life.

THOUGHT FOR THE DAY

As children of God we are expected to go onto maturity. Part of this maturing is growing in our ability to hear, recognize, and see God and His activity.

How have you been developing your "spiritual senses"? In which areas are you seeing growth and in which areas do you think you need to be strengthened in your life?

_____

_____

_____

_____

Spend time in prayer this week, asking God to open your eyes to see where He is working around you; to open your ears to hear His words to you; and to open your heart that you would be ready to respond to His invitation to join Him.

REVIEW YOUR MEMORY VERSE
FOR THE WEEK.

If anyone _____ *Me, let him* _____ *Me; and where I am, there My servant will be also. If anyone* _____ *Me, him My Father will* _____. JOHN 12:26

DAY 3
YOU MUST CLEARLY KNOW HIM

A person must clearly and unmistakably know God. Jesus said eternal life was coming to "know You, the only true God, and the Jesus Christ whom You have sent" (John 17:3). This means you clearly have come to receive Jesus Christ into your life as your personal Savior and Lord.

Take a moment to look back at Unit 3, Day 1. Find the Amplified version of John 17:3 and Philippians 3:10. Record what the words "to know" mean here.

_____

_____

_____

_____

_____

How well have you come to "know"

your Lord in the past few weeks? Are you enjoying the fellowship with your Father in heaven? Are you progressively becoming more deeply and intimately acquainted with Him, perceiving and recognizing and understanding [the wonders of His Person] more strongly and more clearly? Record your thoughts here.

_____

_____

_____

_____

_____

Jesus sought to teach the disciples of His identity from the first miracle of His ministry. However, it was almost three years into Jesus' ministry before Jesus finally asked them, "who do you say that I am?" (Matthew 16:15). When Peter responded that He was the Christ, the Son of the Living God, Jesus assured him that "flesh and blood has not revealed this to you, but My Father who is in heaven" (Matthew 16:17). Only then, with the disciples fully committed to who He was, was He able for the first time to introduce them to His cross, and His coming death (Matthew 16:21).

As you grow in your walk with the Lord, you will come to know Him more personally. When God's people experience His provisions, they often give Him a new name that describes that aspect of God. How have you come to know the Lord? Is He your Provider, your Deliverer, your Advocate?

Jesus is described many different ways in the Scriptures. Select at least three of the names of Jesus below and describe how you have come to understand Christ in that manner (these are only a few of His names).

- ❑ Advocate (1 John 2:1)
- ❑ Almighty (Revelation 1:8)
- ❑ Alpha and Omega (Revelation 1:8)
- ❑ Author and perfecter of our faith (Hebrews 12:2)
- ❑ Bread of life (John 6:48)
- ❑ Captain of salvation (Hebrews 2:10)
- ❑ Christ the power of God (1 Corinthians 1:24)
- ❑ Christ the wisdom of God (1 Corinthians 1:24)
- ❑ Counselor (Isaiah 9:6)
- ❑ Deliverer (Romans 11:26)
- ❑ Door (John 10:7)
- ❑ Eternal life (1 John 5:20)
- ❑ Faithful and True (Revelation 19:11)

- ❑ Friend of sinners (Matthew 11:19)
- ❑ Gift of God (John 4:10)
- ❑ The Savior (Isaiah 45:15)
- ❑ Great shepherd of the sheep (Hebrews 13:20)
- ❑ Judge (Acts 10:42)
- ❑ Light of the world (John 8:12)
- ❑ Lord God Almighty (Revelation 15:3)
- ❑ The Lord, your Redeemer (Isaiah 43:14)

_____

_____

_____

_____

_____

_____

_____

_____

_____

_____

Now look through the list and see if there are some names of Christ that you have not come to understand and experience. List these names and spend some time

asking God to teach you more of who He is through these names.

_____

_____

_____

_____

_____

_____

Without this God-given understanding of who Jesus is, all else is useless. It is essential to the Father's plan. But it is not merely "head knowledge." It must be settled in the heart! The heart determines every response to God. Our own response to God determines how we live out the call and how much more we come to know and experience Him.

THOUGHT FOR THE DAY

Every believer must have a thorough, God-given, personal and ever increasing relationship with Jesus Christ — they must know Him. The entire Christian life depends on it!

Write out your testimony, and describe

how you have been growing in your understanding and fellowship with Christ from the time of your salvation. Be prepared to share this with others from your group this week.

_____

_____

_____

_____

_____

_____

_____

_____

DAY 4
ACCOUNTABILITY TO GOD

Just as simply as a little child, you must daily believe Him. That is, "he who comes to God must believe that He is, and that He is a rewarder of those who diligently seek Him" (Hebrews 11:6). This is because "without faith it is impossible to please Him" (Hebrews 11:6). Therefore, the believer must accept as true all God has revealed about Himself in Scripture. Recognizing that the biblical claims of Christ for His disciples are binding upon his or her life.

With all his or her heart, mind, soul, and strength, a child of God loves Him, and therefore trusts Him, and responds unconditionally to Him. This does not mean we do this perfectly. But, that the aim and desire of your heart is constantly seeking to honor and be acceptable to God.

In 2 Corinthians 5:9–11, Paul expresses his sense of accountability to God. Read

this Scripture and write down in your own words how Paul describes his sense of accountability to God.

_____

_____

_____

_____

Jesus had clearly indicated to His disciples (see Matthew 25) that there would be a time of accountability with God. It is a serious time before God. And He will reward everyone according to his faithful obedience to the Master. Some will hear his Lord say, "Well done, good and faithful servant; you have been faithful over a few things, I will make you ruler over many things. Enter into the joy of your lord" (Matthew 25:23).

Often, this accountability is seen most clearly at our place of employment. I remember talking with a friend named Jim who had been thinking of retiring from his job at the hospital. He shared with his boss his plans and at the same time two floor managers also announced their retirement. With the change in leadership, Jim's boss asked if he would stay longer and direct two floors of the hospital. He shared with his boss that he was ready to retire, but knew that as a Christian he could not simply leave the hospital at such a critical time. Therefore, he changed his retirement and stayed another year.

Jim started at the hospital as a nurse and was determined that he would honor God through his work and always try to leave a good witness. The hospital clearly recognized his work ethic and integrity and God honored him over his 26 years of service. He shared that he always got to work early and stayed late. As a minister in the same city, and often at the hospital where Jim worked, it was obvious that Jim clearly lived out his faith in Christ at work. He honored the Lord with his work ethic, his attitude toward his patients, his bosses, and those who worked for him. It was clear that God had placed this wonderful Christian man in the hospital to be an ambassador for Christ to those hurting and under great physical stress. You see Jim understood that he was accountable to God as a Christian nurse. He recognized that God had placed him at this hospital, and at some point he would have to give an account to his Lord for the way he conducted himself at work.

Read 1 Corinthians 15:10 and Colossians 3:23–24 and describe Paul's sense of accountability and urgency to honor

God in the call He had placed on his life.

_____

_____

_____

_____

It is certainly clear that our accountability is not just at the Judgment, but in this life also. As we are faithful in a little, He gives us more. Take time to meditate on Matthew 25:14–30.

How would you describe your account-ability to God?

_____

_____

_____

_____

What would God say to you if He came today to "settle accounts"?

_____

_____

_____

_____

THOUGHT FOR THE DAY

To live without a real sense of accountability is to lose a major motivation in serving our Lord! Just to know that not a thing we do goes without His notice and love brings comfort. To love Him with all our heart, soul, mind, and strength brings with it such an intimate relationship and spontaneous, joyful accountability. All those who have been greatly used of God lived this way.

Describe how your accountability to God is motivating you in fulfilling God's call on your life.

_____

_____

_____

_____

REVIEW YOUR MEMORY VERSE FOR THE WEEK.

_If anyone _____ Me, let him _____ Me; and where _____ _____, there My _____ will be also. If anyone _____ Me, him My Father will _____. JOHN 12:26_

DAY 5
YOU MUST OBEY HIM

We must have a mindset to obey God immediately. Jesus said, "If anyone loves Me, he will obey My teaching. My Father will love him, and We will come to him and make Our home with him. He who does not love Me will not obey My teaching" (John 14:23–24 NIV).

The Holy Spirit, your enabler, will assist you in hearing, knowing, and living out the call of God. He will do this all throughout your life.

Read the following Scriptures and describe how the Holy Spirit will help you to follow God's call on your life.

John 14:26

_____

_____

_____

Romans 5:3–5

_____

_____

_____

_____

Romans 8:26

_____

_____

_____

_____

1 Corinthians 2:10

_____

_____

_____

_____

Explain how you have been allowing the Holy Spirit to guide you in knowing and living out the call of God in your life.

_____

_____

It is an encouraging thought to know that as we obey God and His call on our lives, the Holy Spirit has been assigned to help us to honor God. Often we can get discouraged or afraid when we see the assignment ahead of us. However, it is important to realize that we are only instructed to follow one step at a time and be concerned with one day at a time. Remember that Jesus has warned us not to worry about tomorrow (Matthew 6:34) but simply take each day and turn it over to the Lord. For example, you may be sensing that God is calling you to teach the Bible to others (which we have already learned is a sign of maturing in Christ), but you may have never taught or led out in this before. God will not simply thrust you into ministry without preparing your life first. He may provide an opportunity to share at a Bible study or share a testimony at church first. He may place you in a class with a teacher who will mentor you and help you know how to study and share the truths of God. Remember that God is faithful to prepare you for the assignment that He is calling you to do.

God may have already been preparing you for an assignment and you have been unaware of this preparation. Look back over your life to see if God has been training you for an opportunity to serve. If you can see how God has been preparing you, describe your preparation in the space below.

_____

_____

_____

_____

_____

_____

_____

_____

Within the church family, the spiritual atmosphere is created where a Christian can hear the call of God and respond confidently. Here, the call of God is clarified and the Christian is assisted to obey God's call.

⟺⟫⟸

Within the church family, the Christian can hear the call of God and respond confidently. Here, the call of God is clarified and the Christian is assisted to obey God's call.

It is in the midst of serving our Lord that His call is clarified. When His call is clarified, we can respond with obedience!

The missions organizations of your church or other groups have a key role in creating this spiritual atmosphere, so that every believer can live out his or her call. Missions organizations provide opportunities for Bible study, mission study, missions activities, personal involvement, models for missions, and ministry and service opportunities. It is, therefore, in the midst of serving our Lord that His call is clarified. When His call is clarified, we can respond with obedience!

Linda and Renee came to our association as volunteer missionaries. They had sensed the call of God to come and spend two years with us. During these two years, we sought to create a spiritual atmosphere in which God would have the maximum opportunity to reveal to each of them the next step in His claim on and call for their lives. We spent time in Bible study and answering questions. They were given assignments that they sensed were from the Lord, and they responded eagerly.

We walked with them through the disappointments, failures, victories, and the painful and happy times.

When their assignment ended, Renee went on to other missions assignments and then to seminary training in preparation for a life of ministry. Linda went to Calgary, Alberta, to direct a ministry at the Winter Olympics, then to serve as a missionary in New York and Atlanta. Currently, she is ministering in Alaska.

The how of being called of God came for both Renee and Linda in the midst of their personal relationship with God and His people as they followed their Lord daily.

THOUGHT FOR THE DAY

Everything in the Christian's life rests on obedience! It unlocks the activity of God in a believer's life. Obedience is the essential heart of experiencing a life on mission with God in the world.

Spend some time before the Lord and ask Him if you have been faithful to obey all He has been asking you to do. Can you describe how your obedience to God is unlocking the activity of God

in and through your life? Or, are there areas of your life where you have not fully surrendered to God and obeyed Him? Write down what God tells you about your obedience to Him and His claim on your life.

_____

_____

_____

_____

_____

_____

_____

REVIEWING WEEK FOUR

Look back over this week's lesson. Pray and ask God to reveal one (or more) statements or Scriptures that He wants you to understand, learn, or practice. **Write it on the lines below.**

_____

_____

_____

_____

_____

_____

Reword the statement or Scripture into a prayer of response to God.

_____

_____

_____

_____

What does God want you to do in response to this week's study? (Take a moment to record this on the "Final Thoughts Summary" found on p. 284–285.)

_____

_____

_____

_____

_____

_____

_____

_____

_____

Review this week's memory verse. Turn it into a prayer of response to God.

_____

_____

_____

_____

PUTTING ASIDE HER FEARS

Rebecca was a very shy person, so shy that she hardly spoke in her college Sunday School class. After graduating from college, she felt God was calling her to be an adult sponsor for a World Changers group. She was assigned to drive a group of young people around for the week. Because of her shyness, she was very afraid to go and wanted to back out. Many of her friends surrounded her and prayed for her the night before she was scheduled to leave. Finally, she realized that God had called her to go on the trip and that she needed to put aside her fears and trust God. She stepped out in faith, and as a result God radically changed Rebecca's life.

Upon returning home, she felt led to apply for a short-term missions assignment. She was accepted and assigned to East Asia, where her job was to build relationships and teach English. As she built relationships at the school, over the Christmas season the school asked her to explain Western culture by reading the Christmas story over the loudspeaker to the entire campus. Rebecca was amazed at how much fun she had serving the Lord in a foreign land.

When the assignment ended, she returned home and sensed a call into full-time Christian service. She is now serving as a career missionary in East Asia. Rebecca's life of service to the Lord and living out God's call on her life began when she set aside her fears and stepped out in faith, believing Her Lord would take care of her. The trust that the Lord built in her heart with a small assignment of driving a vanload of youth has blossomed into an incredible journey of service to her Lord.

UNIT FIVE
WHEN AM I CALLED?

MEMORY VERSE FOR THE WEEK

However, when He, the Spirit of truth, has come, He will guide you into all truth; for He will not speak on His own authority, but whatever He hears He will speak; and He will tell you things to come. He will glorify Me, for He will take of what is Mine and declare it to you. JOHN 16:13–14

ESSENTIAL TRUTH FOR THE WEEK

God is God! When He speaks, He also ensures that you will hear and will know His call. Your heart will be revealed in your response to Him.

No one can come to Me unless the Father who sent Me draws him; and I will raise him up at the last day. JOHN 6:44

He who has My commandments and keeps them, it is he who loves Me. And he who loves Me will be loved by My Father, and I will love him and manifest Myself to him. JOHN 14:21

If anyone loves Me, he will keep My word; and My Father will love him, and We will come to him and make Our home with him. JOHN 14:23

MELVIN AND CARRIE WELLS

TESTIMONY FROM HENRY BLACKABY ABOUT HIS WIFE'S PARENTS

Melvin worked as a salesman for Sears for many years. Carrie worked as a nurse and enjoyed helping people in her church and neighborhood. As a couple, they served faithfully in their church in a wide variety of ministries. Melvin was a deacon and Sunday School director, while Carrie taught youth and was actively involve with the women's missions group in her local church and throughout the region where they lived. As Melvin approached retirement, they sensed God had a special purpose for their retirement years. So, in their late 50s, God led them to use the rest of their lives in overseas missions. They immediately applied to their denomination's mission board and were appointed as missionary associates to Zambia, where they served faithfully into their 60s.

Melvin was a "natural salesman" (from his experience with Sears), and soon was in charge of promoting the Bible Way correspon-

dence courses in this region. He enrolled tens of thousands of people in Bible study courses — many became Christians. He also was given oversight of a church to give counsel to the deacons and leaders to strengthen the churches. Carrie used her nursing skills almost every day and enjoyed building relationships with the native people as well as other missionaries in the region.

One of the most significant assignments they received was when they were asked to become houseparents for missionaries' children. Melvin helped build the residences, and Carrie became an "adopted mother" to many children whose parents were serving God as missionaries across Africa. When they retired from missions work, they returned to the United States and continued serving their Lord. They both remained active in their local church — serving where ever God directed them to serve.

In the midst of these ordinary lives that God used, all three of their children became involved in missions too: their eldest daughter, JoAnn Wells Hopper, spent years with her husband in Eastern Europe (before the Berlin wall came down); their other daughter, my wife, Marilynn, served in Canada with me in church planting; and their son, Melvin Wells Jr., served in Singapore, at the Canadian Baptist Semi-

nary, and is now teaching at Dallas Baptist University (in his retirement years).

Melvin and Carrie were ordinary people who recognized a clear call from God, obeyed immediately, and were used of God, even in their "later" years.

DAY 1
KNOWING THE CALL

As we study the lives of those God used significantly, we notice that it is when we are in the middle of God's activity in our world that we most clearly know the call of God for our lives. A most significant verse to help us understand this is found in the life and witness of Jesus. He said:

> *But Jesus answered them, "My Father has been working until now, and I have been working."* . . . *Then Jesus answered and said to them, "Most assuredly, I say to you, the Son can do nothing of Himself, but what He sees the Father do; for whatever He does, the Son also does in like manner. For the Father loves the Son, and shows Him all things that He Himself does; and He will show Him greater works than these, that you may marvel."* JOHN 5:17, 19–20

What did Jesus say He was doing when

the Father revealed His plan?
❑ Waiting anxiously
❑ Pouting and disillusioned
❑ Already working

Why does the Father show the Son what He is doing?
❑ To confuse Him
❑ So that the Son can join Him in His work
❑ To show Him a better way

When the Father reveals what He is doing, how does Jesus respond?
❑ He does nothing
❑ He acknowledges Him, but continues "business as usual"
❑ He immediately obeys and joins the Father in His work

First, Jesus said that it was the Father who was at work in the world. Jesus was His chosen servant. Jesus said the Son (servant) does not take the initiative, but rather watches to see where the Father (Master) is working and joins Him. Jesus said the Father loves the Son, and therefore shows Him everything that He Himself is doing. The Son joins the Father, working together with Him. It is then that the Father is able to

211

complete all He has purposed to do through the Son. This is how God purposed to bring a lost world back to Himself. He does it through His Son, who loves, trusts, and obeys the Father.

This same pattern is true for how the Father involves us in His work today. Because of the relationship of love between the Father and Christians, He will show us where He is working. When He shows us His work, we must be quick to join Him and, in turn, become workers together with Christ. The example of the life of Christ reveals that it may be costly to join God as He reveals His work. Yet, the end results always glorify God and His purposes. Listen to what the Scriptures say concerning the enormous price God and His Son paid for this great salvation.

Who, in the days of His flesh, when He had offered up prayers and supplications, with vehement cries and tears to Him who was able to save Him from death, and was heard because of His godly fear, though He was a Son, yet He learned obedience by the things which He suffered. And having been perfected, He became the author of eternal salvation to all who obey Him.
HEBREWS 5:7–9

What was the end result of Jesus joining God when the Father revealed His activity?

_____

_____

_____

It cost Jesus His life, on the Cross! Every person through whom God is able to work mightily has lived out this kind of relationship with God.

> *Amos, the prophet, was a shepherd and a caretaker of sycamore-fig trees. He said, I was no prophet, nor was I a son of a prophet, but I was a sheepbreeder and a tender of sycamore fruit. Then the Lord took me as I followed the flock, and the Lord said to me, "Go, prophesy to My people Israel."* AMOS 7:14–15

God had an urgent message that His people needed to hear immediately! Time was running out for them. Judgment was very near. Amos was the man God chose to take His message to His people. It surprised Amos, but he responded obediently, and God accomplished His purposes through him. Though they did not heed His message, they did know God had spoken to them through Amos.

Have you ever felt like Amos when He said, "I was no prophet, nor was I a son of a prophet"? Often we quote the first part of Amos's words but do not follow through with the obedience of Amos.

If God has called you, obey immediately! The safest place you and your family can be is in the center of God's will.

God also called and used Jeremiah in a similar way. Though the pattern is very similar, the messenger is different. Listen to what happened:

Then the word of the Lord came to me, saying: "Before I formed you in the womb I knew you; Before you were born I sanctified you; I ordained you a prophet to the nations." Then said I: "Ah, Lord God! Behold, I cannot speak, for I am a youth." But the Lord said to me: "Do not say, 'I am a youth,' for you shall go to all to whom I send you, and whatever I command you, you shall speak. Do not be afraid of their faces, for I am with you to deliver you," says the Lord. Then the Lord put forth His hand and touched my mouth, and the Lord said to me: "Behold, I have put My words in your mouth. See, I have this day set you

over the nations and over the kingdoms, to root out and to pull down, to destroy and to throw down, to build and to plant." More- over the word of the Lord came to me, saying, "Jeremiah, what do you see?" And I said, "I see a branch of an almond tree." Then the Lord said to me, "You have seen well, for I am ready to perform My word."
JEREMIAH 1:4–12

Have you ever felt like Jeremiah and stated "I am only a youth" and cannot speak or stand before the people? God is not looking for all of your qualifications or abilities; He is looking for your obedience. He will give you the words, the opportunities, and the ability, but He wants you to give Him your trust, faith, and willingness to serve.

God would speak clearly and forcefully to His people through Jeremiah. But the heart of God knew long before Jeremiah was even born that He had "set him apart" for this important time in history. God knew that this time was critical for His people so He revealed His plan to Jeremiah at this time in history. God wanted both a long and a passionate pleading from His heart to come to His people. Jeremiah was then shaped by God to be the one through whom He would speak.

God has found messengers through whom He could speak and work in every generation in history. Some of the most significant include Moses, the Judges, David, all the prophets, the disciples, the apostle Paul, and many more of God's people throughout history. This God-chosen process continues to this very day and is the way God will call and work through your life, too. God has worked and moved throughout history to accomplish His eternal purpose. Always, eternity is in the balance. Those He chooses, calls, shapes, and uses are painfully and deeply aware of "this assignment." They are the clay and God is the potter. God always has a design in mind when He chooses a person.

Moreover God said to Moses, "Thus you shall say to the children of Israel: 'The Lord God of your fathers, the God of Abraham, the God of Isaac, and the God of Jacob, has sent me to you. This is My name forever, and this is My memorial to all generations.'" EXODUS 3:15

Has God called you to an assignment where you have felt inadequate to serve? What excuses have you been using to stop you from obeying?

_____

_____

Hopefully by now you are coming to understand that God only wants your heart and
availability to Him. He can and will shape
you for the assignment, but He needs you
to step out and allow Him access to fashion
your life for use in His eternal plan.

**Read Jeremiah 18:1–6 to see how God
desires to shape a life for His service.
List some of your discoveries here.**

_____

_____

_____

_____

**Based on this Scripture, can you see
how God has been shaping your life?
Explain how God has been shaping your
life recently.**

_____

_____

_____

_____

_____

_____

_____

THOUGHT FOR THE DAY

Those God chooses and calls know it is God, know what He is saying, and know how they are to release their lives to Him for His purposes in their day!

What assignment are you deeply aware of that God has given you in the last month and how have you released your life to be used for His purposes?

_____

_____

_____

_____

_____

_____

DAY 2
A DAILY WALK, THOROUGHLY REARRANGED

When God sees a growing, loving, and responsive relationship of trust in Him by one of His children, He continues His call on that person's life. He usually does this in the midst of a person's daily routine. Through this daily routine, God calls a person to a special relationship with Him. It is also remarkable that the daily response of each person brings the enabling presence and power of the Spirit of God.

For example, God placed His Spirit on the responsive Moses, and later on the 70 elders who were to work with him (read Numbers 11:16–25). The daily walk of Moses with God, guiding His people, was exceedingly demanding for Moses. It would require the full presence and enabling that only the Spirit of God could bring. But God also provided 70 other key leaders who would share his load of leadership. They would require the same Spirit of God. God provided thoroughly, and certainly adequately, for them all. This enabling provided what was needed for the leaders to guide God's people according to His commands and purposes.

Has God placed able people around your life to walk along side of you as a source of help and encouragement? If so, write down their names and how God is using them to strengthen your life. If not, make this a matter of prayer until God brings some of His people around you to walk with you.

_____

_____

_____

_____

_____

Later, God commanded Moses to build a tabernacle for His presence among His people. It would require the utmost care and obedience to all God would direct. God told Moses He had already chosen and placed His Spirit on some men who would do all that He commanded. They were ordinary workmen, chosen by God and equipped by God's Spirit to do His will in all things.

Read Exodus 35:30 to 36:21. What kind of work did God equip the people to do in these verses?

_____

_____

_____

_____

Do you find it surprising that the Spirit equipped them to do building, wood carving, artistic works, tapestry making, and weaving? Often we assume that the Spirit only equips people to preach or teach the gospel. However, God equips His people in a wide range of talents to be used to bring honor to His name. For example, many retired people are being called of God to use their trade skills to travel throughout the year to build churches, repair buildings after disasters, and renovate church camps. To watch these people work and hear their heart for God is to know that they have been anointed by God for His service. Many times the wives of these workmen bring along sewing machines and make clothes for children in need. When you see their work, it becomes clear that Exodus 35:35 — "He has filled them with skill to do all manner of work" — is actively demonstrated throughout their life and ministry.

Has God equipped you with skills that He desires you to use for His service? If so, write them down below and write a prayer of commitment that the skills He has given to you are now available for His service.

_____

_____

_____

_____

This pattern of God working through ordinary people, called, assigned, and enabled by God, continued through each of the Judges of Israel. Each was called at a crucial moment in the life of God's people when they needed deliverance from their enemies. David's life follows this same pattern (read 1 Samuel 16:13); the disciples and the Apostle Paul were also shaped and used by God in their day.

⸺⸺⸺

God has huge purposes to accomplish through His people in our day . Our world is changing, and God is orchestrating His people to accomplish His purposes.

Now it is our turn. This is especially true because God has huge purposes to accomplish through His people in our generation. Our world is changing, and God is orchestrating His people for His purposes. But oftentimes they are not in a spiritual condition to respond to Him! So once again, God is looking for someone who will "stand in the gap before Me on behalf of the land, that I should not destroy it" (Ezekiel 22:30).

So much is in the balance, especially in light of eternity. The heart of God has not changed. He is not willing that any should perish, but that all should come to repentance (2 Peter 3:9). So in this our day, and in your life and mine, it is still incredibly true:

For the eyes of the Lord run to and fro throughout the whole earth, to show Himself strong on behalf of those whose heart is loyal to Him. 2 CHRONICLES 16:9

So the process continues. But now it involves you, and it involves me! And God is watching to see how we will respond to Him.

THOUGHT FOR THE DAY
The key to being used by God is the con-

dition of our heart and our willingness to respond in obedience to His call on our life. Our usefulness to God does not rest in our abilities or talents or in the lack of them, but in our availability.

Why is the condition of a person's heart and not one's abilities the basis on which God chooses to use a person?

_____

_____

_____

_____

REVIEW YOUR MEMORY VERSE FOR THE WEEK.

However, when He, the _____ of _____, has come, He will _____ you into all _____; for He will not speak on His own authority, but whatever He _____ He will _____; and He will tell you things to come. He will Me, for He will take of what is Mine and declare it to you. JOHN 16:13–14

DAY 3
COMPLETELY ENABLED

As already mentioned, the one God calls, He also thoroughly equips to enable them to respond in every matter toward God. God is on mission and the servant of the Lord must "be where the Master is." And Jesus added significantly, "If anyone serves Me, him My Father will honor" (John 12:26).

———

God is on mission and the servant of the Lord must "be where the Master is."

———

Whole books could be written just on this intimate relationship between the Lord and His servants. But the enabling provision of God for His servants is clearly declared and seen throughout Scripture and history. Some of the "provisions of God" are clear.

Read the following Scriptures and write down what they state about God's provision for His people.

2 Corinthians 1:20

_____

_____

_____

_____

Philippians 4:19

_____

_____

_____

_____

2 Peter 1:3–4

_____

_____

_____

_____

The greatest of God's provisions is His Holy Spirit. Jesus assured His disciples, "You shall receive power when the Holy Spirit has come upon you" (Acts 1:8). He had earlier assured them, "And I will pray the Father, and He will give you another Helper, that He may abide with you forever — the Spirit of truth" (John 14:16–17).

The Holy Spirit is God Himself, present and active, enabling every believer to do whatever God commands. He would always let them know the Father's will for each of them (John 16:13; 1 Corinthians 2:9–16). He would guide them into all truth, teach them all things, and bring to their remembrance everything Christ had commanded them (John 14:26; John 16:13–15). He would also help them when they prayed (Romans 8:26), something that would be so much a part of their relationship to God and His will in their lives. And, the Holy Spirit would work the Scriptures into their lives as a "sword" (Ephesians 6:17–18).

Those God used in the Old Testament had the Spirit come upon them to totally enable them. In the New Testament, every believer would have the Spirit of God at conversion. But more significantly, the Holy Spirit would "fill" those whom God called to be available to Him as He took His great salvation message to the whole world.

⎯⎯⎯⎯

Now it is our turn. All that was available to people in Scripture is available today to every believer called of God. No matter what it is that God commands the believer to do with Him, His provision is already present and available, and the Holy Spirit is actively working to implement all of it into that believer's life. No matter how "difficult or impossible" an assignment God places on the life of one of His children, God's provision will completely enable them to do it.

God's provision for every believer on mission with God is the fullness of His presence. In His presence we are "complete" (Colossians 2:9–10). Every believer is enabled to experience God finishing His work through them (Philippians 1:6). The Holy Spirit does this in many ways.

Read Colossians 2:9–10 and Philippians 1:6. How do these Scriptures shape your understanding of God's equipping for your ministry?

_____

_____

_____

One way of enabling comes as the believer spends time in God's word. In the midst of the study, the Holy Spirit gives a confirming "Yes" to what He knows to be the will of God. It comes as a quiet assurance, giving peace and joy. He also gives affirmation when the believer takes time to pray and seek assurance from God of His will. To the carefully observant person who prays, there comes a quiet direction to the prayer, putting the person into the center of the will of God (read Romans 8:26–28). When John was praying on the island of Patmos, the Holy Spirit gave him clear direction concerning the will of God (read Revelation 1).

What affirmations and enabling has God brought to your life from prayer and Bible study this past month?

_____

_____

_____

_____

Throughout history, the witness of those used of God indicates that some of the great affirmations of God have come to them in prayer. Further affirmations of God come by what He is doing around the believer, and in the midst of His people, the local church.

If you sense you know God's will, and yet do not see God doing what He promised, God may be seeking to tell you that either you are not in His will or that His timing is not always immediate.

It is important to keep in mind that God can and does affirm His will for His servants. If God does not express Himself toward you, He may be trying to let you know something else. When God promises something, He does it. If you sense you know God's will, and yet do not see God doing what He promised, God may be seeking to tell you that either you are not in His will (read Isaiah 46:11*b;* Isaiah 14:24, 27; 1 Kings 8:56) or that His timing is not always immediate. God may be taking the time necessary to develop character in your life before He can give you all He has planned for you. Ask God and He will guide you to know the truth of your situation.

THOUGHT FOR THE DAY

God has promised incredible affirmation of His will and His call in our lives. It is important that each believer be constantly alert to God's word of confirmation, however He chooses to express it. But never go long without some affirmation from the Lord that you are in the center of His will.

Describe how God has confirmed that you are currently in the middle of His will and are faithfully fulfilling His call upon your life.

_____

_____

_____

_____

_____

Day 4
Necessity of Functioning in the Body

Being involved in the local church creates a wonderful opportunity to understand the call of God. The most complete descriptions of how the body functions together are found in 1 Corinthians 12, Ephesians 4, and Romans 12.

Each member in the body functions where God places him or her in the body, and each assists the other parts of the body to grow up into the Head, which is Christ. This is not merely a figure of speech; it is a living reality. The loving Christ is truly present in the church body, and each member really does assist the others to know and do the will of God. Paul constantly affirmed his need of other believers to help him know and carry out the call of God in his life.

For I long to see you, that I may impart to you some spiritual gift, so that you may be established — that is, that I may be encour-

232

aged together with you by the mutual faith both of you and me. ROMANS 1:11–12

And [pray] for me, that utterance may be given to me, that I may open my mouth boldly to make known the mystery of the gospel, for which I am an ambassador in chains; that in it I may speak boldly, as I ought to speak. EPHESIANS 6:19–20

Describe how your life is currently encouraging others in their faith in the church you attend.

_____

_____

_____

_____

_____

_____

_____

_____

_____

_____

Are you letting others in your church encourage your life? How are you doing this?

_____

_____

_____

_____

In the church where God places you He has provided other believers, whom He has equipped, to assist you in recognizing God's call and activity in your life. These people will pray for you, encourage you, and assist you in carrying out His will.

~~~

Your life in the body of Christ is crucial if God is to carry out His eternal purpose for your life today.

~~~

The body of Christ is a crucial part of God's plan to carry out His eternal purpose for your life. The eye can assist the ear to know what it is hearing, the hand as to what it is feeling, and the feet where to step next. The life of the body is affected by each member relating in love to one another (Ephesians 4:16).

This will involve you not only in your church family but also with the other churches in your local area, across the nation, and around the world. God's call is to take the gospel to every person and into every nation. God's plan for accomplishing this is to call you to Himself, and then place your life alongside all the others He has called, so that together, as one people, He can work dramatically across an entire world!

THOUGHT FOR THE DAY

God's call in your life always includes your intimate involvement with His people in and through your local church.

Read Ephesians 4:1–16 and prayerfully consider the following questions. How does God want to use you in the church where He has placed you?

_____

_____

_____

_____

_____

Are you allowing Him to use you in this manner?

_____

_____

_____

_____

However, when He, the _____ of _____, has come, He will _____ you into all _____; for He will not _____ on His own _____, but whatever He _____ He will _____; and He will tell you things to come. He will _____ Me, for He will take of what is _____ and declare it to _____. JOHN 16:13–14

DAY 5
COMPLETE AFFIRMATION

God through love affirms His presence and
His call in your life daily! The heart that
seeks Him, finds Him; the life that asks
Him, receives; to the one who knocks, God
opens a door (Matthew 7:7–11). God responds to His children, and they know that
it is God who is affirming their relationship
with Him.

**The heart (life) that is earnestly seek-
ing Him will daily spend time in God's
Word.** When we do, the Holy Spirit uses
the word of God like a sword (Ephesians
6:17) to convict us of sin, to lead us into "all
truth," to teach us "all things," to bring to
our remembrance all that Christ has been
saying to us, and to help us thoroughly understand and apply His will and call to our
lives (John 14:26; 16:7–15).

As a believer opens the Scripture, the
Holy Spirit is present and actively seeking
to bring the earnest seeker into the will of

God. Words suddenly have new meanings and seem to apply directly to our life. This is the affirmation of God in our life through the working of the Holy Spirit. The same is true of all Scripture, in particular the life and teachings of Jesus. "All Scripture is given by inspiration of God, and is profitable for doctrine, for reproof, for correction, for instruction in righteousness" (2 Timothy 3:16). Throughout the entire process, the Holy Spirit "bears witness with our spirit," not only that we are children of God, but that we are in the center of the will of God (Romans 8:16, 27).

The person with a heart seeking after God will also spend much time in prayer. God has given the Holy Spirit the responsibility to guide each of us into the will of God as we pray (Romans 8:26–27). Too often, our prayer begins quite self-centered and self-focused! As we continue to pray, soon our prayer turns God-centered. This is the Holy Spirit at work, according to the will of God. Follow the Spirit's directives immediately and completely.

You may be praying with anger, even resentment, against someone or some situation. Soon God's love fills your heart, and your prayer changes to expressions of love and blessing. This is God. He has affirmed not only His presence but also His will toward your life. Thank Him and alter everything into His directives, for He is ready to bless you greatly!

⊰※⊱

Sometimes God uses friends or family or persons in your church to give you affirmation for your call.

⊰※⊱

Sometimes God uses friends or family or persons in your church to give you affirmation for your call. Someone shares a Scripture with you that is the very same Scripture God gave you that morning. This is God's affirmation! A timely phone call or letter comes — again, God's affirmation to your life and call. A caution, or even a word of correction becomes God's affirmation not to proceed.

Remember, there are no coincidences in the life wholly yielded to God! God is completely involved in the life of the one He calls to go with Him. But there is an additional word to share at this point. If you see NO affirming presence of God in your life or ministry, you need to stop and see if indeed you may be out of God's will. The lack of affirmation may be due to sin or rebellion in your life.

⸺⊶⸻

There are no coincidences in the life wholly yielded to God! God is completely involved in the life of the one He calls to go with Him.

⸺⊶⸻

THOUGHT FOR THE DAY

God never leaves His children to guess whether they are walking in the center of His will. He provides plenty of daily assurances! As you have been going through this study, you have been challenged to examine God's call upon your life and His desire to use you in the middle of His activity to redeem a lost world. You have been looking at how you are serving in your community, church, and beyond.

What affirmations from God have you received during these past five weeks that you are truly seeking and honoring Him? What Scriptures has He used to assure you of your walk with Him?

_____

_____

_____

_____

REVIEWING WEEK FIVE

Look back over this week's lesson. Pray and ask God to reveal one (or more) statements or Scriptures that He wants you to understand, learn, or practice. **Write it on the lines below.**

_____

_____

_____

_____

Reword the statement or Scripture into a prayer of response to God.

_____

_____

_____

_____

What does God want you to do in response to this week's study? (Take a moment to record this on the "Final Thoughts Sum-

mary" found on p. 284–285.)

_____

_____

_____

_____

_____

_____

_____

Review this week's memory verse. Turn it into a prayer of response to God.

_____

_____

_____

_____

_____

_____

_____

_____

_____

_____

ROB BRANDT

More Comfortable Behind the Scenes

Often, we see the examples of heroes from the Bible or well-recognized people from Christian history, but fail to recognize that the mission of God is most often accomplished through "ordinary" people like you and me. We could give you countless stories of wonderful people that will not been known or recognized outside of their circles of influence until they hear "Well done, good and faithful servant" from their Lord.

Rob served faithfully, but quietly at his church. He had resisted the church's request to become a deacon, but after much prayer, he and his wife agreed to serve as a deacon couple. Rob and his wife loved the Lord deeply, and also had a heart to help people (especially those who did not "fit in"). It seemed that every Sunday they had a new person or couple sitting with them at church. They would explain how they met this person at a store or through work and invited them to church and most often to their home for lunch. Rob and his wife had a quiet ministry in the church reaching out to people in the community and bringing them to church (with many coming into a personal relationship with Christ).

Our ministry was asked to conduct an Experiencing God weekend for a church in rural Alberta which included putting together a team of volunteers to help lead group sessions and give personal testimonies throughout the weekend. As we started to ask people to consider joining the team for the weekend, Rob was one of the first people we asked. Rob reluctantly agreed to pray about joining with us on the weekend. While he loved to help people, he did not feel that he was able to help or be a part of this kind of ministry. Rob is a gifted woodworker (he owns a woodworking business) and a maker/collector of custom knives and sword-canes, but he did not feel capable of sharing in front of a church or leading out in a small group. Over the next couple of weeks, Rob wrestled with God over this invitation. He explained that God had been telling him for a while that he needed to step out in faith and take on greater responsibility in ministry. Finally, after much agony and soul-searching, he agreed to come with us.

The team had several people with seminary training and ministry experience; however the person that the church identified most with was Rob. His experiences growing up, background in woodworking, and running his own business, as well as his quiet, but kind manner had an immediate impact on the people. Later, as we evaluated the weekend, it was clear that God had used Rob to make a significant impact on the church. We heard wonderful comments about the teaching and group times, but people continued to make reference to Rob's testimony or something Rob shared that impacted their lives. It was interesting to hear from Rob's perspective — he felt that the weekend was more for him and what God wanted to teach him than it was to share with the church. God knew that He intended to use Rob to impact this church and He began to work on his heart long before we asked him to join our team. However, when Rob accepted the invitation to join God at work he had no idea of the profound impact it would have on his own personal life.

UNIT SIX
HOW DO I LIVE OUT THE CALL?

———————

MEMORY VERSE FOR THE WEEK

For it is God who works in you both to will and to do for His good pleasure. PHILIPPIANS 2:13

ESSENTIAL TRUTH FOR THE WEEK

God's provisions for a relationship with Him are completely thorough. Nothing is missing from God's perspective. What would it take to miss His calling? You would have to resist, quench, and grieve Him, His Son, and His Holy Spirit to miss His call.

CLAY AND LOIS QUATTLEBAUM
SERVING IN RETIREMENT

Clay and Lois first met in university as they were both studying to become schoolteachers. Both of them were committed Christians and they served God faithfully for many years as elementary school teachers in the Southern California public schools. Upon retirement they sensed that God had a new assignment for their lives and ministry.

As they prayed for several months, God began to reveal His plans to them. He was inviting them to come and serve alongside Henry and Marilynn at Blackaby Ministries. We had been friends with Clay and Lois since university. This invitation from God required them to make major adjustments. As we prayed together, and became convinced that this was God's will, Lois and Clay sold their home in Southern California and relocated to Atlanta to work as volunteers with Blackaby Ministries.

This step of obedience caused them to leave a very comfortable retirement, many life-long friends, and a church family they had been a part of for more than 40 years. As they have been serving God at Blackaby Ministries, their servant hearts and their willingness to help have brought great joy to us and countless others. If you were to ask them why they left everything that was familiar to them and moved across the country to serve as volunteers they would say, "Retirement from the public schools didn't mean retirement from serving our Lord!"

DAY 1
DESIRE TO FOLLOW THE CALL

God Himself places within the heart of every believer the deepest desire to experience the strong presence and power of His working in and through them. God will not override your heart or your will, but He will thoroughly influence your life toward His will and His call. Notice this in this Scripture passage: *Therefore, my beloved, as you have always obeyed, not as in my presence only, but now much more in my absence, work out your own salvation with fear and trembling; for it is God who works in you both to will and to do for His good pleasure.* Philippians 2:12–13

What are the two things that God is working in your life as a believer?

_____

_____

_____

_____

But how does one come to experience the deep reality of being called and accountable?

As we look for the answer to this question, it is important to remember that not only is it "God who works in you both to will and to do for His good pleasure" (Philippians 2:13), but also, "He who has begun a good work in you will complete it until the day of Jesus Christ" (Philippians 1:6). This is a wonderful verse to encourage us to never quit or give up because God is always faithful to finish the work and complete all He desires to do through our lives if we will let Him.

In Paul's letter to the church at Ephesus, he prayed for them that they would not miss out on all that God had provided for them. Certainly this included the wonderful blessing of living out the call of God in their lives as individuals and as a church family.

Read Ephesians 3:14–21 and answer the following questions. As you read, remember that Paul's prayer is that God would grant all of these things according to the riches of His glory. Can you imagine the vast enormity of God's riches? According to each of the following verses, what does Paul ask God to grant to the Ephesian church?

Verse 16

_____

_____

_____

Verse 17

_____

_____

_____

Verse 18

_____

_____

_____

Verse 19

_____

_____

_____

What is God's ability to give or bless in our lives, according to verse 20?

_____

_____

_____

When God fulfills the things listed in verses 14–20, where does He receive the glory according to verse 21?

_____

_____

_____

_____

THOUGHT FOR THE DAY

The inner desire to know God's call and to completely do it is granted to every believer.

Describe how God is placing a desire in you to know and live out the call.

_____

_____

_____

_____

REVIEW YOUR MEMORY VERSE FOR THE WEEK.

For it is God who _____ in you both to _____ and to _____ for His good pleasure. PHILIPPIANS 2:13

DAY 2
INVOLVING YOUR CHURCH IN THE CALL

As you live out your life, God will cultivate a deep desire within you to follow Him and allow Him to accomplish His plan through you. This is the activity of God in your life causing you to want to do His will. The activity of God may be experienced while you are studying the Bible, when you are worshipping in your church, when you are praying, in the midst of your daily routine, even when you are talking with a friend or family member. There are some things that only God can do. Creating awareness of His call is something only God can do in a believer's life.

———

There are some things that only God can do.

———

Here are a few examples.

Bill and Anne responded very differently than other people in our community when we learned that a policeman in our city had been murdered. The two young men who committed the crime were arrested, and the anger of the people in the city mounted. But during our prayer meeting, Bill and Anne began to weep as they shared a deep burden in their hearts for the parents of the two young men arrested. They themselves had a son in jail, and they knew the pain and loneliness of being the parents. As they shared their hearts, the entire church family began to understand and feel their pain too. We knew God was trying to speak to us through them.

Bill and Anne asked that we pray for them because they had invited the parents of these two boys to their home for coffee. They had shared their concern with these parents and confirmed God's personal love for them. As a church, we agreed to pray for Bill and Anne as they sought to minister to these families.

The parents of the two boys cried out, "We have been hated and cursed by others. You are the only people who have cared about how much we are hurting. Thank you!"

Out of this experience, our church family, along with Bill and Anne, began an extensive jail ministry — to both the inmates and the parents and family in several jails and prisons. The entire church became involved. Why? Because two believers knew they were children of a loving God and knew that God was calling them to respond. God wanted to work through them and their church in the lives of others who were hurting. One of our mission churches was even begun with families of prison inmates.

Another woman, Cathy, joined our church. The prayer meeting became a very special place for her. In the meetings, as she prayed, she often sensed the moving of God in her life, giving her clear direction.

One Wednesday evening she shared, "God has given me a great burden for ministering to the mentally and physically disadvantaged and their families. I grew up with a mentally handicapped sister. I know what this does to the parents and the family. No one in the churches of our city is ministering to these people. I sense we should seek God's guidance to see if we should be involved." The more she shared and the more we prayed, the more our hearts came together as one (Matthew 18:19–20).

We became convinced that God was directing not only Cathy but also our entire church to become involved. To us it was a clear call of God, and we felt accountable to God to respond. We did, and Cathy helped us know what to do. Soon we had 15 to 20 mentally challenged young adults attending church with us along with some of their family members. Our church came to experience more of the meaning of pure love through these special people than we had ever experienced before. God called Cathy and her church as she prayed (and then we prayed with her), and God began to accomplish His loving purposes through us.

These are two examples of how God spoke to an individual who shared God's call on their life with their church. And just as Paul prayed in Ephesians 3, God received glory in the church as the whole body of believers helped these individuals live out the call. Living out the call of God will involve those around you. Take a moment to read the Scriptures listed here. Record your responses to the questions.

Read Matthew 18:19–20. What does God promise to those who gather together and live out the call of God on their lives?

_____

_____

_____

What do each of these Scriptures say about how Christians are to relate to each other as they serve God together?

Romans 12:16

_____

_____

_____

_____

1 Corinthians 1:10

_____

_____

_____

_____

1 Peter 3:8–9

_____

_____

_____

_____

Philippians 2:2

_____

_____

_____

_____

THOUGHT FOR THE DAY

God will not let you "miss" His call on your life or your church when you are intentionally listening to Him and abiding in His love. God often uses your local church family to help you understand His call as well as live out this call.

How is God using your Christian family to understand His call? Can you describe how your Christian family is helping you to fulfill this call?

_____

_____

_____

_____

REVIEW YOUR MEMORY VERSES.

_And whatever you do, do it _____, as to the _____ and not to _____, knowing that from the _____ you will_

receive the _____ of the inheritance;
for you serve the _____ _____.
COLOSSIANS 3:23–24

And this is _____ _____, that
they may _____ You, the _____
_____ _____, and
_____ _____ whom You have
sent. JOHN 17:3

DAY 3
BEARING WITNESS
TO THE CALL

Terry worked for a very significant micro-chip company. As Terry studied his Bible, prayed, and worshipped regularly, God began to speak to him. During a worship service, Terry came forward indicating that God was calling him to be a more effective witness in his place of work.

"But," he said, "my desk is out of the way at the end of a hall and only one person comes by my office. How can God use me to witness to the people in my office?"

I shared his sense of call with the church, and we pledged to pray with him. I encouraged him to look carefully for the activity of God in answer to our prayer and to be prepared to obey immediately. It was not long before he joyfully shared with the church: "This week my boss came to me and said, 'Terry, I want to move your desk. I hope you don't mind!' My desk now is in the busiest place in the office, right beside the drinking fountain, the copier, and the coffee center. Everybody comes by my desk now. Please pray for me that I will be the faithful witness God has called me to be in my workplace!"

―――――

When we bear witness to the call of God and then live out the call among God's people, it will serve as an encouragement to others to step out in faith to serve God.

―――――

His experience caused the entire church to be more sensitive to God's call in their lives. When we bear witness to the call of God and then live out the call among God's people, it will serve as an encouragement to others to step out in faith to serve God. Because of those who were living out the call in the fellowship of our church, many significant purposes of God were worked out over the next year.

Can you see how important it is to bear witness to the call of God and testify to how He is causing you to live out this call? Let's look at a few examples of this truth from the Scriptures.

How did the news of the way Philemon was living out the call of God among the church impact Paul's life? (Philemon 7)

_____

_____

_____

_____

Would someone describe you as *one who refreshes* hearts?
❑ Yes
❑ No

What did the testimony of the Colossian church cause Paul to do toward God? (Colossians 1:3)

_____

_____

_____

_____

Why do you think Paul continually shared with the early churches about the way in which he was living out the call of God? (Philippians 1:12–18; 1 Thessalonians 2:1–12; 1 Timothy 1:12–17)

_____

_____

_____

_____

Paul was careful to share his life and call with the early church to encourage them, to set an example, and to stir them to follow the call of God in their own lives. Many times people around you have a desire to follow God but are afraid to step out in faith. As you follow God, share how God is working in your life so that it will serve as a source of encouragement to others who may be hesitant to release their own life to God.

—⸙—

As you follow God, share how God is working in your life so that it will serve as a source of encouragement to others who may be hesitant to release their own life to God.

—⸙—

THOUGHT FOR THE DAY

Sharing your calling with your church and living out this call among the fellowship of the church will serve as an encouragement to the entire church body.

265

Can you think of a person in your church or circle of influence whose life and devotion to Christ serves as a source of encouragement to the rest of the group? How has their life impacted your own life?

_____

_____

_____

_____

In what ways have you allowed your life to serve as an encouragement to others to follow after Christ?

_____

_____

_____

_____

REVIEW YOUR MEMORY VERSES.

The _____ *of the Lord run* _____ _____ _____ *throughout the whole earth, to show Himself* _____ *on behalf of those whose* _____ *is* _____ *to Him. 2* CHRONICLES 16:9

If anyone _____ Me, let him _____ Me; and where _____ _____, there My _____ will be also. If anyone _____ Me, him My Father will _____. JOHN 12:26

DAY 4
DAILY LIVING

How do you live out the call of God in your life? It begins and is sustained in your daily relationship with God, from the beginning of the day to the end of the day!

David's life is a great example of one who followed the Lord. Read Psalm 63 and then answer the following questions.

What words does David use to describe the way He sought the Lord? (v. 1)

_____

_____

_____

_____

When did David meditate on God? (v. 6)

_____

_____

_____

According to this psalm, what were the reasons David sought after God from early morning to late into the night?

_____

_____

_____

_____

David stated that his soul thirsted for God, that he desired to see His power and glory (vv. 1–2); he longed to experience God's loving-kindness (v. 3) and to have his soul satisfied by God (v. 5), because God was his help (v. 7), and David had found protection under God's wing (v. 7).

Can you see why David would seek after God in the process of living out his life as God's servant? God continues to watch over His people, and those who have come to walk intimately with God throughout the day and night can identify with David in this psalm.

In your quiet time, when you are alone with God, God will speak to you and guide you to understand and know what He is planning to do through your life. If you close this time by saying, "O God, please go with me this day and bless me!" God may say to you, "You have it backwards! I have a will and plan for what I want to do through your life today. I want you to go with Me. So I am alerting you now through My Word and your praying to know My will for you, so you can be partners with Me today!" A by-product of partnering with God each day is knowing that you are with Him and experiencing His best.

⟞⟊⟐⟊⟝

It is not what you can do for God, but what God is doing in you!

⟞⟊⟐⟊⟝

In your quiet time, the Lord will bring His full assurance that whatever the Father has in mind, He (Jesus) will be present with you and in you to provide all the resources you will need to see the Father's will fulfilled. In addition, the Holy Spirit will enable you to implement the specific will of God. What an incredible privilege! What an awesome responsibility! What an accountability we have to love Him, believe Him, trust Him, and obey Him. It is then that you will experience the wonderful presence and power of God working His will in you and through you.

As a result, because you know that God is working in you and will complete what He has begun, you should live with a clear sense of expectation and anticipation. It is not what you can do for God, but what God is doing in you! And what He begins, He Himself will bring to completion. How encouraging it is to read in Isaiah a promise from God:

The Lord of hosts has sworn, saying, "Surely, as I have thought, so it shall come to pass, and as I have purposed, so it shall stand. For the Lord of hosts has purposed, and who will annul it? His hand is stretched out, and who will turn it back?" ISAIAH 14:24, 27

When you read this verse, does it give you confidence that the Lord who called you will complete everything He has purposed to do in and through your life?

Do you have any current decisions to make in your walk with God but you have been hesitant to step out in faith because you cannot foresee the outcome? If so, write the decisions below and then ask God to apply this passage

in Isaiah to your situation.

_____

_____

_____

_____

_____

_____

_____

Once God has spoken to your heart, it is as good as done. For God has never spoken to reveal His will and not Himself guaranteed the completion of what He has said. This will be as true for you as for anyone in the biblical history.

⟞⟝

God has never spoken to reveal His will and not guaranteed the completion of what He has said.

⟞⟝

Read the following Scriptures and write down how they describe God and how He fulfills His Word and completes

His work. Once you have studied these Scriptures, ask God to apply them to current events and decisions you are facing.

Isaiah 55:6–13

_____

_____

_____

_____

Numbers 23:19

_____

_____

_____

_____

How confident can you be that the Lord will fulfill all He has purposed for your life based on these Scriptures?

_____

_____

_____

_____

THOUGHT FOR THE DAY

You can be absolutely confident that once God has begun a work in you or revealed where He wants you to join Him in His work, He will be faithful to carry the work to its completion.

Based on the Scriptures of today's study, write down in your own words how you would explain to another person why a Christian can completely trust God as he answers God's call upon his life.

_____

_____

_____

_____

REVIEW YOUR MEMORY VERSES.

However, when He, the _____ of _____, has come, He will _____ you into all _____; for He will not _____ on His own _____, but whatever He _____ He will _____; and He will tell you things to come. He will _____ Me, for He will take of what is _____ and declare it to _____. JOHN 16:13–14

For it is _____ who _____ in you both to _____ and to _____ for His good _____. PHILIPPIANS 2:13

But now I come to You [the Father], and these things I speak in the world, that they may have My joy fulfilled in themselves. JOHN 17:13

DAY 5
THE JOY OF LIVING OUT THE CALL OF GOD

So often we look at the call of God on our lives and tend to focus on the work ahead or the sacrifices involved. While there is much labor involved and many sacrifices along the way, these things do not compare to the joy that comes from following the call of God.

Jesus urged the disciples to remain or abide in His love by keeping His commandments, and by doing this they would remain in the love of the Father (John 15:9–10). However, He went on to say that the reason He was telling them to do this was so that His joy would remain in them and that their joy would be full (John 15:11). When we follow God's leading in our life and submit ourselves to His will, the result is that we experience the joy of Christ in our lives. In John 17:13, Jesus states that He was praying for the disciples and speaking to the Father so that they would have His joy fulfilled in their lives.

*But now I come to You [the Father], and
these things I speak in the world, that they
may have My joy fulfilled in themselves.*
JOHN 17:13

**Have you recognized that Jesus desires
to see your life filled with His joy?**

_____

_____

**Can you describe your life today as
filled with His joy because you have
sought to remain in His love and obey
His commands?**

_____

_____

**Would others recognize that your obe-
dience to Christ has produced an out
flowing of joy in your life? If not, why
not?**

_____

_____

_____

There is also great joy that comes from living
out the call in the midst of God's people. If
you think back over the times you have been

overwhelmed with joy, or excited because of something good, most often you can hardly wait to tell others the good news. It is wonderful to be able to share good things with others. There is an excitement to serve God together as His "called out" people.

———

Everyone became involved in God's activity, individually as well as corporately as a body, with God.

———

Among God's people, we have experienced the excitement of being on mission. Ministry to the down-and-out, to the school system, to the jails, to the mentally and physically handicapped, to the university, to the reservations, to the surrounding towns and villages, and even to the ends of the earth was experienced by the members of our church. Everyone became involved in God's activity, individually as well as corporately as a body. Many felt called to be pastors or church staff; others felt called to minister in other countries of the world; still others gained a clear sense of a call to serve, witness, and minister in the marketplace and the homes where God had placed them. Together we helped each other to be accountable — first to God who had called us and then to each other as we sought to be a body of Christ in our world. Overall, the greatest joy comes as we realized the God of the universe could and would carry out His purposes through us.

There is great joy that comes when you are on mission with God and with His people! And along with this joy comes a great accountability to God. Certainly the parable of the talents found in Matthew 25:14–30 is a warning. We will give an account for all God has called us to do and equipped us to accomplish. Paul challenged the Corinthians that each one's work or service to God would be made clear before God.

Each one's work will become clear; for the Day will declare it, because it will be revealed by fire; and the fire will test each one's work, of what sort it is. If anyone's work which he has built on it endures, he will receive a reward. If anyone's work is burned, he will suffer loss; but he himself will be saved, yet so as through fire.
1 CORINTHIANS 3:13–15

A call to salvation is a call to be on mission

with our Lord. This call was not just for a select few but to all who were called to a relationship with Christ. How tragic it would be for a Christian to waste the one life and opportunity to be a co-worker with Christ (and miss the rewards) only to be saved as through fire, but carry no heavenly rewards of following the call.

<hr/>

A call to salvation is a call to be on mission with our Lord. This call was not just for a select few but to all who were called to a relationship with Christ.

<hr/>

Read 2 Corinthians 5:10. Have you been living your life with the understanding that one day you will give an account for how you used your life, either in service to God or looking out for self?

_____

_____

_____

_____

_____

How has this understanding shaped the way you order your goals and priorities?

_____

_____

_____

_____

_____

THOUGHT FOR THE DAY

Answering the call of God brings great joy to a Christian's heart. This joy is experienced individually in one's heart, but also corporately, as Christians are privileged to serve God together in their local church setting.

REVIEWING WEEK SIX

Look back over this week's lesson. Pray and ask God to reveal one (or more) statements or Scriptures that He wants you to understand, learn, or practice. Write it on the lines below.

_____

_____

_____

_____

_____

_____

_____

_____

Reword the statement or Scripture into a prayer of response to God.

_____

_____

_____

What does God want you to do in response to this week's study? (Take a moment to record this on the "Final Thoughts Summary" found on p. 284–285.)

_____

_____

_____

_____

Review this week's memory verse. Turn it into a prayer of response to God.

_____

_____

_____

_____

CONCLUSION

The call of God is a call to an exciting relationship with God for the purposes He had for us from before the foundation of the world. God calls us by causing us to want to do His will and then enabling us to do it. He first calls each of us to be His child by faith in Jesus, His Son. In that relationship, God has provided all we need to live fully with Him. That relationship will always involve us in His redemptive activity in our world. In that relationship, God Himself will work through us in our world. As God works through us in our world, we will come to know Him and grow toward Christlikeness. A Christlike character is God's preparation for eternity with Him. What a plan and what a purpose God has for each of us! May we respond to Him as He works in us and through us mightily in our world.

Called and accountable — God's greatest of privileges given freely to every believer!

FINAL THOUGHTS SUMMARY STATEMENTS

Week 1

_____

_____

_____

_____

Week 2

_____

_____

_____

_____

Week 3

_____

_____

_____

_____

Week 4

_____

_____

_____

Week 5

_____

_____

_____

_____

Week 6

_____

_____

_____

_____

CALLED AND ACCOUNTABLE
LEADER'S GUIDE

HOW TO USE THIS LEADER'S GUIDE

If you are leading *Called and Accountable* as a group study, this leader's guide will help you plan for group meetings. These two pages provide generic guidelines; refer to them when using the planning pages for each unit.

Before Each Session

1. Complete all five days of the unit during your daily quiet times.
2. Pray, asking the Spirit's guidance for the session. Be right with God, confessing any known sin, so you may be a pure vessel for Him to use, excited to share truth. Pray for each group member.
3. Prepare specifics for leading the ses-

sion by filling in the "During the Session" page for the unit.

4. Attend to any logistical issues, such as arranging the meeting place (including DVD setup), posting signs, planning for refreshments, contacting group members, or gathering needed materials.

5. Make your own checklist in the space provided for you.

   ❑ _____

   ❑ _____

   ❑ _____

   ❑ _____

Welcome and Opening Prayer *(10 minutes)*
Watch Video *(15 minutes approximately)*
Testimony *(5 minutes)*
Truths *(10 minutes)*
Questions *(15 minutes)*
Summary & Challenge *(5 minutes)*
Next Week *(5 minutes)*
Closing Prayer *(10 minutes)*
During the Session _____

1. **Welcome and Opening Prayer:** Plan to welcome members and open with a short time of prayer. As group members become closer, allow time for

sharing prayer requests before prayer.

2. **Watch Video Segment:** You may want to watch the video before each session. See the DVD menu details for planning.

3. **Questions/Insights from Testimonies:** Plan questions or comments for a brief discussion of the *Called & Accountable* testimonies for the week, found at the beginning and end of each unit. (Unit 6 has one testimony and a conclusion.) Possible questions: How did you respond to the testimonies? What was unusual about them? Has God ever called you in such a way?

4. **Major Truths of Study:** Plan to bring out the main truths of the unit by reviewing and discussing the Essential Truth for the Week and the Thoughts for the Day.

5. **Discussion Questions Drawn from Study:** Develop questions to lead the group to listen to what God is teaching them through their study. Focus on creating readiness for learning, reinforcing important truths, and stimulating personal application. Possible questions:

   ✓   What did God say to you as you studied this unit?

✓ What were some statements in the workbook that were particularly important to you?

✓ What adjustments is God asking you to make?

6. **Summary/Challenge:** Summarize the important learning that was experienced by the group in this session. Challenge them to be diligent in completing the daily studies and in praying.

7. **Create Anticipation:** Prepare the group for the next session by creating anticipation for the new unit. Take a moment to read the "Essential Truth" for the upcoming week.

8. **Closing Prayer:** Pray for the group before they leave, using Scriptures and their applications from the group discussion.

PLANNING PAGES FOR UNIT ONE

Before the Session

1. Complete all five days of the unit during your daily quiet times.
2. Pray, asking the Spirit's guidance for the session. Be right with God, confessing any known sin, so you may be a pure vessel for Him to use, excited to share truth. Pray for each group member.

3. Prepare specifics for leading the session by filling in the "During the Session" page for the unit. Adapt the suggested segments to your group's needs.

4. Attend to any logistical issues, such as arranging the meeting place, posting signs, planning for refreshments, contacting group members, or gathering needed materials.

5. Make your own checklist:

❑ _____

❑ _____

❑ _____

❑ _____

Welcome and Opening Prayer *(5 minutes)*
Watch Video *(15 minutes)*
Testimony *(5 minutes)*
Truths *(10 minutes)*
Questions *(10 minutes)*
Summary & Challenge *(5 minutes)*
Next Week *(5 minutes)*
Closing Prayer *(5 minutes)*
During the Session _____

1. Welcome/Opening Prayer:

_____   _____

_____   _____

Prayer Requests:

_____ _____

_____ _____

_____ _____

_____ _____

2. Questions/Insights from Testimonies:

_____ _____

_____ _____

_____ _____

_____ _____

3. Major Truths of Study:

_____ _____

_____ _____

_____ _____

_____ _____

4. Discussion Questions Drawn from Study:

_____ _____

_____ _____

_____ _____

5. Summary/Challenge:

_____ _____

_____ _____

_____ _____

_____ _____

6. Create Anticipation:

_____ _____

_____ _____

_____ _____

_____ _____

7. Closing Prayer:

❑ _____

❑ _____

❑ _____

❑ _____

PLANNING PAGES FOR UNIT TWO
Before the Session _____

1. Complete all five days of the unit during your daily quiet times.
2. Pray, asking the Spirit's guidance for the session. Be right with God, confessing any known sin, so you may be a pure vessel for Him to use, excited to share truth. Pray for each group member.

3. Prepare specifics for leading the session by filling in the "During the Session" page for the unit. Adapt the suggested segments to your group's needs.

4. Attend to any logistical issues, such as arranging the meeting place, posting signs, planning for refreshments, contacting group members, or gathering needed materials.

5. Make your own checklist:

   ❑ _____

   ❑ _____

   ❑ _____

   ❑ _____

Welcome and Opening Prayer (5 minutes)
Watch Video (15 minutes)
Testimony (5 minutes)
Truths (10 minutes)
Questions (10 minutes)
Summary & Challenge (5 minutes)
Next Week (5 minutes)
Closing Prayer (5 minutes)
During the Session _____

1. Welcome/Prayer:

_____ _____

_____ _____

Prayer Requests:

___ _____

___ _____

___ _____

___ _____

2. Questions/Insights from Testimonies:

___ _____

___ _____

___ _____

___ _____

3. Major Truths of Study:

___ _____

___ _____

___ _____

4. Discussion Questions Drawn from Study:

___ _____

___ _____

___ _____

___ _____

5. Summary/Challenge:

_____ _____

_____ _____

_____ _____

_____ _____

6. Create Anticipation:

_____ _____

_____ _____

_____ _____

_____ _____

7. Closing Prayer:

☐ _____

☐ _____

☐ _____

☐ _____

PLANNING PAGES FOR UNIT THREE

Before the Session _____

1. Complete all five days of the unit during your daily quiet times.
2. Pray, asking the Spirit's guidance for the session. Be right with God, confessing any known sin, so you may be

a pure vessel for Him to use, excited to share truth. Pray for each group member.

3. Prepare specifics for leading the session by filling in the "During the Session" page for the unit. Adapt the suggested segments to your group's needs.

4. Attend to any logistical issues, such as arranging the meeting place, posting signs, planning for refreshments, contacting group members, or gathering needed materials.

5. Make your own checklist:

❑ _____

❑ _____

❑ _____

❑ _____

Welcome and Opening Prayer (5 minutes)
Watch Video (15 minutes)
Testimony (5 minutes)
Truths (10 minutes)
Questions (10 minutes)
Summary & Challenge (5 minutes)
Next Week (5 minutes)
Closing Prayer (5 minutes)
During the Session _____

1. Welcome/Opening Prayer:

_____   _____

_____   _____

Prayer Requests:

_____   _____

_____   _____

_____   _____

2. Questions/Insights from Testimonies:

_____   _____

_____   _____

_____   _____

3. Major Truths of Study:

_____   _____

_____   _____

4. Discussion Questions Drawn from Study:

_____   _____

_____   _____

_____   _____

5. Summary/Challenge:

_____   _____
_____   _____
_____   _____
_____   _____

6. Create Anticipation:

_____   _____
_____   _____
_____   _____
_____   _____

7. Closing Prayer:

❑   _____
❑   _____
❑   _____
❑   _____

PLANNING PAGES FOR UNIT FOUR

Before the Session _____

1. Complete all five days of the unit during your daily quiet times.
2. Pray, asking the Spirit's guidance for the session. Be right with God, confessing any known sin, so you may be

a pure vessel for Him to use, excited to share truth. Pray for each group member.

3. Prepare specifics for leading the session by filling in the "During the Session" page for the unit. Adapt the suggested segments to your group's needs.

4. Attend to any logistical issues, such as arranging the meeting place, posting signs, planning for refreshments, contacting group members, or gathering needed materials.

5. Make your own checklist:

❑ _____

❑ _____

❑ _____

❑ _____

Welcome and Opening Prayer *(5 minutes)*
Watch Video *(15 minutes)*
Testimony *(5 minutes)*
Truths *(10 minutes)*
Questions *(10 minutes)*
Summary & Challenge *(5 minutes)*
Next Week *(5 minutes)*
Closing Prayer *(5 minutes)*
During the Session _____

1. Welcome/Prayer:

_____ _____

_____ _____

Prayer Requests:

_____ _____

_____ _____

_____ _____

_____ _____

2. Questions/Insights from Testimonies:

_____ _____

_____ _____

_____ _____

3. Major Truths of Study:

_____ _____

_____ _____

_____ _____

_____ _____

4. Discussion Questions Drawn from Study:

_____ _____

_____ _____

_____ _____

_____ _____

5. Summary/Challenge:

_____ _____

_____ _____

_____ _____

_____ _____

6. Create Anticipation:

_____ _____

_____ _____

_____ _____

_____ _____

7. Closing Prayer:

❑ _____

❑ _____

❑ _____

❑ _____

PLANNING PAGES FOR UNIT FIVE
Before the Session _____

1. Complete all five days of the unit during your daily quiet times.

2. Pray, asking the Spirit's guidance for the session. Be right with God, confessing any known sin, so you may be a pure vessel for Him to use, excited to share truth. Pray for each group member.

3. Prepare specifics for leading the session by filling in the "During the Session" page for the unit. Adapt the suggested segments to your group's needs.

4. Attend to any logistical issues, such as arranging the meeting place, posting signs, planning for refreshments, contacting group members, or gathering needed materials.

5. Make your own checklist:

   ❑ _____

   ❑ _____

   ❑ _____

   ❑ _____

Welcome and Opening Prayer (10 minutes)
Watch Video (15 minutes)
Testimony (5 minutes)
Truths (10 minutes)
Questions (10 minutes)
Summary & Challenge (5 minutes)
Next Week (5 minutes)
Closing Prayer (5 minutes)

1. Welcome/Prayer:

_____ _____

_____ _____

   Prayer Requests:

_____ _____

_____ _____

_____ _____

_____ _____

2. Questions/Insights from Testimonies:

_____ _____

_____ _____

_____ _____

_____ _____

3. Major Truths of Study:

_____ _____

_____ _____

_____ _____

_____ _____

4. Discussion Questions Drawn from Study:

_____ _____

_____ _____

_____ _____

_____ _____

5. Summary/Challenge:

_____ _____

_____ _____

_____ _____

_____ _____

6. Create Anticipation:

_____ _____

_____ _____

_____ _____

_____ _____

7. Closing Prayer:

❑ _____

❑ _____

❑ _____

❑ _____

PLANNING PAGES FOR UNIT SIX

Before the Session _____

1. Complete all five days of the unit dur-

305

ing your daily quiet times.

2. Pray, asking the Spirit's guidance for the session. Be right with God, confessing any known sin, so you may be a pure vessel for Him to use, excited to share truth. Pray for each group member.

3. Prepare specifics for leading the session by filling in the "During the Session" page for the unit. Adapt the suggested segments to your group's needs.

4. Attend to any logistical issues, such as arranging the meeting place, posting signs, planning for refreshments, contacting group members, or gathering needed materials.

5. Make your own checklist:

❑ _____

❑ _____

❑ _____

❑ _____

Welcome and Opening Prayer *(10 minutes)*
Watch Video *(15 minutes)*
Testimony *(5 minutes)*
Truths *(10 minutes)*
Questions *(10 minutes)*
Summary & Challenge *(5 minutes)*

Evaluate *(5 minutes)*
Closing Prayer *(5 minutes)*
During the Session _____

   1. Welcome/Opening Prayer:

_____   _____

_____   _____

       Prayer Requests:

_____   _____

_____   _____

_____   _____

   2. Questions/Insights from Testimonies:

_____   _____

_____   _____

_____   _____

_____   _____

   3. Major Truths of Study:

_____   _____

_____   _____

_____   _____

4. Discussion Questions Drawn from Study:

_____ _____

_____ _____

_____ _____

_____ _____

5. Summary/Challenge:

_____ _____

_____ _____

_____ _____

_____ _____

6. Create Anticipation:

_____ _____

_____ _____

_____ _____

_____ _____

7. Closing Prayer:

❑ _____

❑ _____

❑ _____

❑ _____

PARTICIPANT/VIEWER NOTES

_____

_____

_____

_____

_____

_____

_____

_____

_____

_____

_____

_____

_____

_____

ABOUT THE AUTHORS

Henry T. Blackaby is the author of *Experiencing God,* which has sold more than 7 million copies and has been translated into some 50 languages. He describes *Called and Accountable* as his sequel to that work. Henry is president of Blackaby Ministries International, an organization he founded to help people experience God in a more intimate way. Born in British Columbia, he has devoted his lifetime to ministry.

Norman C. Blackaby, professor at Dallas Baptist University, teaches in the PhD program for the Graduate School of Leadership in addition to Old Testament courses for the Biblical Studies program. He holds a PhD in biblical backgrounds and archeology. He has served as a senior pastor at two churches and as vice-president of Blackaby Ministries International for six years. In addition, Norman is the coauthor of *Experiencing Prayer* *with Jesus, Encounters with God: Transforming Your Bible Study, Called and Accountable: Discovering Your Place in God's Eternal Purpose, Called and Accountable 52-Week Devotional,* and a contributor to *The Blackaby Study Bible* and the "Encounters with God" book study series.

The employees of Thorndike Press hope you have enjoyed this Large Print book. All our Thorndike, Wheeler, and Kennebec Large Print titles are designed for easy reading, and all our books are made to last. Other Thorndike Press Large Print books are available at your library, through selected bookstores, or directly from us.

For information about titles, please call:
(800) 223-1244

or visit our Web site at:
http://gale.cengage.com/thorndike

To share your comments, please write:
Publisher
Thorndike Press
10 Water St., Suite 310
Waterville, ME 04901